MONTANA MAVERICKS

Welcome to Big Sky Country, home of the Montana Mavericks! Where free-spirited men and women discover love on the range...

BROTHERS AND BRONCOS

Romance is in the air for the ranchers of Bronco, but someone is watching from the sidelines. A man from the town's past could be behind the mysterious messages, but does he pose a threat to Bronco's future? With their happily-ever-afters at stake, the bighearted cowboys will do what it takes to protect their beloved town— and the women they can't live without!

THE MAVERICK'S CHRISTMAS SECRET

After months in town, ranch hand Sullivan Grainger seems no closer to discovering what really happened to the brother he never knew. When he asks gift shop owner Sadie Chamberlin for help, falling for her is the last thing he expects—or wants. Sadie knows she is in over her head, but she can't shake the feeling that she and the lonesome cowboy are meant to be...

Dear Reader,

Confession: I'm one of those people who likes to have my Christmas tree up and decorated by December 1 because I want to enjoy and celebrate the holiday season for as long as possible. (And, of course, my halls—and every room in my house—are decked with more than boughs of holly.)

But nobody in Montana is a bigger fan of Christmas than Sadie Chamberlin, who spreads cheer year-round through Holiday House in Bronco Valley. And all her customers leave the shop with smiles on their faces—except Sullivan Grainger.

The rancher is new in town—he's come to Bronco to learn everything he can about Bobby Stone, the twin brother he never knew who went missing three years earlier, so it's no wonder he isn't in the mood for celebrating. But spending time with Sadie, whose sister was once married to his brother, Sullivan can't help but find himself enchanted by the magic of the season—or at least by the pretty shopkeeper.

As the days count down toward December 25, Sadie helps Sullivan not only embrace the holiday but also understand that "family" means the people you love and home really is where your heart is.

Wishing you love and joy this festive season and always,

xo *Brenda*

The Maverick's Christmas Secret

BRENDA HARLEN

HARLEQUIN
SPECIAL
EDITION

Special thanks and acknowledgment are given to Brenda Harlen for her contribution to the Montana Mavericks: Brothers & Broncos miniseries.

Recycling programs for this product may not exist in your area.

ISBN-13: 978-1-335-72431-1

The Maverick's Christmas Secret

For questions and comments about the quality of this book, please contact us at CustomerService@Harlequin.com.

Harlequin Enterprises ULC
22 Adelaide St. West, 41st Floor
Toronto, Ontario M5H 4E3, Canada
www.Harlequin.com

Printed in U.S.A.

Brenda Harlen is a former attorney who once had the privilege of appearing before the Supreme Court of Canada. The practice of law taught her a lot about the world and reinforced her determination to become a writer—because in fiction, she could promise a happy ending! Now she is an award-winning, RITA® Award–nominated, nationally bestselling author of more than fifty titles for Harlequin. You can keep up-to-date with Brenda on Facebook and Twitter, or through her website, brendaharlen.com.

Books by Brenda Harlen

Harlequin Special Edition

Match Made in Haven

A Chance for the Rancher
The Marine's Road Home
Meet Me Under the Mistletoe
The Rancher's Promise
The Chef's Surprise Baby
Captivated by the Cowgirl
Countdown to Christmas

Montana Mavericks: Brothers & Broncos

The Maverick's Christmas Secret

Montana Mavericks:
The Real Cowboys of Bronco Heights

Dreaming of a Christmas Cowboy

Montana Mavericks: What Happened to Beatrix?

A Cowboy's Christmas Carol

Montana Mavericks: Six Brides for Six Brothers

Maverick Christmas Surprise

Visit the Author Profile page
at Harlequin.com for more titles.

For Susan Litman,
who has wrangled every one of my books
from outline to publication for the past twenty years,
with many thanks and much appreciation.

(Yes, it's been that long—and yes, I know
she's just dying to take a red pen to that dedication.)

Prologue

If he wanted to learn about Bobby Stone, he needed to talk to the people who knew him. And wasn't that the reason he'd come to Bronco in the first place? Even though, almost five months later, Sullivan Grainger still didn't have any of the answers he sought.

Today, that was going to change.

He paid for his purchase and exited Bean & Biscotti, then stood on the sidewalk, nibbling on a sugar twist and sipping his coffee as he studied the festive window across the street at Sadie's Holiday House.

The display was set up like a living room decorated for the holidays. At the center was an electric fireplace, the mantel draped with natural evergreen garland with "snow-dusted" pinecones and red berries, and half a dozen assorted stockings. To one side of the fireplace was a red-velvet wing chair and a small table with a brass lamp. A plush white throw embossed with silver snowflakes was draped over the back of the chair and on the table was a pile of books—all with holiday titles. On the opposite side of the fireplace was a Christmas tree, beautifully decorated with colorful lights and ornaments. Brightly wrapped presents were piled beneath it.

A sign on the door counted down the number of days until Christmas—30—and in the short time that it took him to eat his donut and drink his coffee, he watched several shoppers make their way in and out of the store—most of them exiting with more bags than they'd carried when they'd entered. Apparently, the residents of Bronco were almost as big on celebrating the holidays as his mother.

Adoptive mother, he mentally amended.

Though he'd only recently discovered *that* truth. And while it wasn't easy to get over the sense of betrayal and let go of the resentment, he was trying.

He tossed his now-empty coffee cup in the garbage can on the sidewalk, crossed the street and pulled open the door of Sadie's Holiday House.

A musical chime, like the sound of sleigh bells, announced his arrival, though he doubted it was audible to Sadie Chamberlin, the store's proprietor, over the Christmas music playing.

From the bits and pieces that he'd been able to gather around town, Sadie was the sister of Bobby Stone's ex-wife. And so Sullivan had decided that she would be a good source for insight about his missing brother.

He passed a man and a woman each carrying a

bag stamped with the shop's logo. He recognized the woman as Brynn Hawkins and the man as one of the many Abernathys who populated Bronco. Garrett, he guessed, since he'd heard talk around town that the eldest of Hutch and Hannah's sons had been keeping company with the stunning rodeo rider.

Garrett did a double-take as they passed, but Sullivan didn't pause. He moved purposefully into the shop, toward an attractive young woman with long, wavy blond hair who was tidying a display of nutcrackers.

She looked up at his approach. When she met his eyes, her easy smile slipped and all the color drained from her face. Then she let out a startled cry and crumpled to the ground.

Lunging forward, Sullivan managed to catch her just before she hit the floor.

In the movies, the heroines always seemed to faint slowly, giving the hero plenty of time to swoop in and catch them.

This one had dropped like a bag of rocks.

But she didn't feel like a bag of rocks, he acknowledged. She was soft and warm, and it had been a long time since he'd had a woman in his arms. This one was really pretty, too. And she smelled good. Like apple cider and gingerbread. Or maybe it was the candles around the shop that smelled of those things.

"Bobby?"

The query came from Garrett, who'd paused at the door.

Sullivan, still holding the shopkeeper, glanced over

his shoulder to shake his head. "No. But I understand why you might think that."

Sadie finally started to stir.

Her eyelids flickered then opened to reveal warm, dark brown eyes. She lifted a hand to touch his cheek. "Bobby? Is it really you?"

"No," he said again, feeling sincerely regretful that his response was going to disappoint her. "But I guess we really do look the same."

He heard Garrett murmur something to Brynn, though they were too far away for him to make out the words. And anyway, he had his hands full—*literally*—with Sadie Chamberlin.

"You and Bobby could be twins," Sadie responded weakly.

His mouth twisted in a wry smile. "Funny you should say that."

Her brow furrowed. "I don't understand."

He intended to tell her everything—or at least as much as he knew—but right now, he had a more immediate concern.

"Should I call 9-1-1?" he asked.

"What?" She blinked. "Why?"

"Because you fainted," he reminded her.

A tinge of color returned to her cheeks. "I did, didn't I? I'm so sorry. I've never done anything like that before. If anyone had asked, I would have said for certain that I wasn't the type of woman who fainted. Then again, I've never before felt as if I was face-to-face with a ghost."

"Is that a *yes* or *no* about 9-1-1?" he prompted.

"No." She seemed to realize she was still in his arms and pulled away, rising to her feet and reaching out a hand to steady herself on one of the display cabinets. "I'm fine. Really."

"Are you sure?"

"I'm sure. I just…" She lifted her gaze to his again. "It was a shock, that's all. It's still a shock," she admitted. "You just…you look so much like Bobby."

And Sullivan finally spoke aloud the words he'd kept buried deep in his heart for so long: "Probably because he's my twin brother."

Chapter One

Bobby Stone had a twin brother.

Nine days after her first meeting with Sullivan Grainger, Sadie Chamberlin was still reeling from that revelation.

In all the time that Bobby had been married to Sadie's sister, Dana, he'd never mentioned having a twin—or even a sibling. Which wasn't surprising if, as Sullivan suspected, Bobby hadn't known that he wasn't an only child—a truth that the newcomer to town had apparently only recently discovered for himself.

Unfortunately, he hadn't had the opportunity to share much more than that with Sadie before other customers came into Holiday House, requiring her assistance. And for the first time since she'd taken over the shop after Gwendolyn McCormick's passing, Sadie had wished she could shoo the shoppers out of the store, turn the sign from Open to Closed and give Sullivan her full attention.

He'd lingered for a while, pretending an interest in various items on display while she was otherwise occupied. But when it had become apparent that she wasn't going to have even five minutes to sit and chat—because Lynda, one of her regular employees, had called in sick—Sullivan had ducked out.

She didn't blame him, but nine days later, Sadie still had questions she desperately wanted answered. So many questions.

She'd been certain he would come into the shop again, because there had to be a reason that he'd sought her out in the first place. But he didn't return to Holiday House, though a couple of times she'd caught a glimpse through the window of a man she thought might have been him. And as she didn't know where to find him, that reason remained a mystery.

She hoped that she might get lucky today, though, as it was Bobby's birthday—and therefore his twin brother's birthday, too. And because it was a Sunday, the store didn't open until one o'clock, so if their paths did cross, they would hopefully have time enough for a real conversation.

But first, she had wreaths to deliver to Gemstone Diner.

She parked at the back of the restaurant and carried the holiday decorations through the employee entrance, tracking down Wayne Twitchett in his office. She tapped on the partially open door to draw the attention of the diner's owner, who was scowling at his computer screen.

"I've got your wreaths, Mr. Twitchett."

"That's great, Daisy. Thanks."

"It's Sadie," she reminded him, as she did every time their paths crossed and he called her by the wrong name.

"Right—Sadie," he said, gesturing toward a cracked leather sofa on the opposite side of the room. "Just put them over there."

She set the box down.

He went back to scowling at the computer.

"Merry Christmas, Mr. Twitchett."

"Yeah. Thanks. You, too."

She ducked out of his office and cut through the kitchen to the dining area to say a quick hello to her mom, who'd waited tables there every Sunday morning for as long as Sadie could remember.

"The Langleys will be out of here in about two minutes," Roberta said, as she made her way past carrying a tray weighed down with plates of pancakes and waffles and scrambled eggs. "You can grab their table when it's free."

Sadie waited until the meals had been served before she replied, "I can't stay for breakfast this morning."

"Then why are you here?"

"I came to deliver the wreaths Mr. Twitchett ordered—and to say hi to you."

"I've been on Wayne for years about updating the tired holiday decorations in here," Roberta said. "I'm glad to see he finally listened."

"Actually, I'm not sure he did," Sadie cautioned. "I got the impression that his wife wanted the wreaths for their new house."

"I should have realized." Her mom dropped her voice to a near whisper. "They moved to Bronco Heights, you know. Don't pay their servers enough to keep a roof over *their* heads, but the two of them are living in a fancy house with four bedrooms and four bathrooms."

"So quit," Sadie urged quietly. "You don't need this job anymore."

Roberta sighed. "I know. But I like working here— not the job, but the customers," she clarified.

"I know you do," she acknowledged.

Her mom deposited her tray behind the counter. "Do you at least have time for a cup of coffee?"

"I'll take one to go," she decided.

"To go where?" Roberta asked, as she filled a large paper cup, added a splash of cream and a spoonful of sugar, then covered it with a lid.

"I've got another delivery to make this morning," Sadie responded vaguely.

Ordinarily her mom would ask, which made Sadie suspect that Roberta knew where she was going but didn't want to talk about it.

Because while Roberta usually prided herself on being "in the know" with respect to everything happening in Bronco, there were other times when she preferred to be "in denial." And while the rumors that had circulated around town for the past few months about Bobby Stone's ghost had faded into the background as news that newcomer Sullivan Grainger was the missing man's brother had gained steam, her mom had said nothing to Sadie.

She understood that Roberta's former son-in-law was one topic of conversation that she preferred to avoid, because any mention of Dana's ex-husband inevitably made her think about the daughter that she'd lost. So Sadie hadn't said anything, either, and she certainly didn't remind her mom that today was Bobby's birthday.

Instead, she took the coffee her mom offered and tucked a five-dollar bill into her pocket as she kissed her cheek.

What was he doing here?

That was the question Sullivan kept asking himself as he trudged through the fresh snow toward the stone that marked his brother's empty grave.

There should be a better way to remember Bobby on his thirty-ninth birthday, and while lifting a glass to him at Doug's bar came to mind, after the incident a few months back, Sullivan suspected that he might be *persona non grata* at the local watering hole. In any event, it was barely ten o'clock in the morning and unlikely that Doug would be pouring pints at such an early hour on a Sunday.

In fact, most of the town had been quiet as he'd passed through Bronco Valley on his way to the cemetery. The few vehicles that he'd passed on the road seemed to be headed to one of the nearby churches or Gemstone Diner or Bean & Biscotti. He'd made a quick detour to the local café, too, for a cup of coffee that he knew would be much more palatable than what he could get from the little shop attached to the motel that had been his home for the past several months.

When he'd exited Bean & Biscotti, his gaze had automatically drifted to Sadie's Holiday House. Though the shop was closed, the colored lights twinkled on the elaborately decorated tree in the front window.

According to the sign on the door, the countdown to Christmas was now at twenty-one days. Which meant that Sadie had already been at the shop this morning to change the sign—or maybe she'd changed it before she closed up at the end of the previous day, because it had displayed 22 when he'd stopped by on Saturday.

He'd made his way back to the store in the Valley Center shopping district a few times since their initial introduction, but he'd only ventured into the store once more—to buy a holiday wreath for Bobby's grave.

At least, that had been the pretext for his visit. It wasn't until he'd felt a pang of disappointment upon discovering Sadie wasn't in the shop that he'd acknowledged the truth: he'd been looking forward to seeing her again.

According to the young man working the cash register, "the boss" was on her lunch break, eliminating any lingering hope that she might pop out of one of the back rooms at any moment. Sullivan could have gone back to the shop later in the day to see if she'd returned, but that would have seemed a little too obvious.

Too desperate.

Even if he was eager to see her again and finish the conversation they'd barely started.

Because, after more than five months in Bronco, he still had too many unanswered questions about his brother's life—and his death.

There were other people in town he could talk to, and he'd made some efforts to do so. When word finally got around that he wasn't Bobby Stone's ghost but his twin brother, some of the locals had been happy to chat with him and share their memories. But it had quickly become apparent that none of them had really known Bobby.

They might have shared a few drinks at Doug's bar on occasion or played a little pool together, but they'd told him nothing about his brother aside from the facts that he was "fun-loving," "easygoing" and "a great mechanic." It was also unanimously agreed that Bobby was "still hung up on his ex-wife" when he'd gone on his fateful hike more than six months after their divorce.

Sullivan would have liked to talk to Dana, to find out what went wrong in their marriage. Unfortunately, that wasn't an option, as she'd been killed in a car accident another six months after Bobby went missing. It was that discovery that had led him to seek out Dana's sister—Sadie Chamberlin.

Maybe he should have anticipated that his physical resemblance to his brother might be a shock to her, but he hadn't imagined that she'd faint at the sight of him. She'd come to quickly, though, and had seemed disappointed to learn that he wasn't Bobby back from the dead but his twin. Or maybe Sullivan was reading too much into her reaction.

In any event, he hadn't been the least bit disappointed to meet Sadie. And though they hadn't had much time to talk, he'd enjoyed making her acquaintance. And her smile.

She had a really sweet smile. And after living in a dark place for the past several months, something about her smile made him feel as if the sun was finally shining again.

But today he wasn't thinking about Sadie Chamberlin or the upcoming holidays, only his brother. He stood in front of the modest headstone inscribed with the name "Robert James Stone" and his date of birth followed by the month and year of his disappearance, as if the answers to all the mysteries of the universe—or at least his brother's life—might be found there.

No one knew exactly when he'd died and Bobby's body had never been found. As a result, Sullivan couldn't help but hope that his brother might not really be gone, though he knew that was only wishful thinking, because there was no way anyone could have survived the fall he'd taken.

He stuffed his hands deep into the pockets of his coat, hating to acknowledge that truth and hating, even more, that he'd never have a chance to know him.

"So why did I feel the need to come to Bronco?" he wondered aloud. "Why am I still here? Why do I feel as if there's something undone?

"And why am I talking to a headstone over an empty plot of land? Because even if you are dead, I know you're not buried here."

He sighed wearily. "Or maybe the answer to that question is as simple as the fact that I don't have anyone else to talk to. I'm still too angry with my adoptive parents to want to talk to them and, despite having been in Bronco for several months, I haven't really made any friends here."

"If that's true, it's only because you haven't tried," a female voice said from behind him.

Sullivan turned abruptly, startled to find himself face-to-face with Sadie Chamberlin.

"I didn't mean to eavesdrop. I just brought this—" she held up the miniature Christmas tree in a shiny red pot that she carried in both hands "—for Bobby."

Any embarrassment he might have felt at being caught talking to a grave was immediately dispelled by her smile.

"It was kind of you to remember him," he said.

"He might have been my brother-in-law for only five years, but he was my friend even after that. And while he wasn't much for flowers, he did like Christmas."

Sadie took a few steps closer, then crouched to set the pot on the ground, on the opposite side of the headstone from which he'd laid the wreath.

"Happy birthday, Bobby," she said quietly. Then she turned to Sullivan again and offered him another small smile. "And happy birthday to you, too."

"Thank you," he murmured. But the fact that she'd remembered her brother-in-law's birthday, more than three years after his disappearance, made him wonder if Sadie might have had a more personal relationship with his twin.

...he was my friend even after that, she'd said.

But maybe they'd been more than friends.

Or maybe discovering that the couple he'd always believed were his parents had lied to him for thirty-eight years had made Sullivan distrustful of everyone and their motives.

Either way, he had questions for Sadie.

A lot of questions.

He cleared his throat. "Actually, I'm glad to see you," he said. "I was hoping you could tell me about my brother's relationship with your sister."

"It's a rather long story," she told him. "Are you sure you want to talk about it here?"

The *here* didn't really matter to Sullivan, but he wanted to talk about it *now*. After months of searching online and more recent inquiries around town, he'd barely scratched the surface of his brother's life, and he was growing desperate for answers.

But as a gust of wind blew across the field, he saw Sadie shiver and tuck her chin into the collar of her coat and acknowledged that this probably wasn't the best place to pursue the answers he sought.

So he tamped down his impatience and said, "You tell me when and where."

"How about over lunch at DJ's Deluxe?" she suggested.

He glanced at his watch. "It's kind of early for lunch, isn't it?"

"Not for people who have to be at work for one o'clock," she said.

"Then we better head over to DJ's to get you some lunch."

But he glanced over his shoulder at Bobby's gravestone one more time before he followed Sadie away.

Chapter Two

Sadie cranked the heat up in her SUV as she drove away from the cemetery and toward the upscale barbecue restaurant in Bronco Heights. As her blood began to thaw, so did her brain, and she immediately began questioning the wisdom of inviting Sullivan Grainger to have lunch with her.

But when she'd seen him there, standing in the snow beside Bobby's empty grave, looking lost and forlorn, her heart had ached for him. It wasn't in her nature to turn away from someone who was hurting, so when she'd realized that he had questions about Bobby's relationship with Dana, she'd wanted to give him the answers—preferably somewhere that she could do so without her teeth chattering.

She'd planned to grab a quick bite before heading to

the shop, and being in the mood for a burger, she'd decided that the Gemstone Diner would fit the bill. But she didn't want to take Sullivan there, because she wasn't sure how Roberta would react to seeing her daughter walk in with a man who was a dead ringer (Sadie cringed at the cliché description even as it popped into her head) for her former son-in-law.

So she'd suggested DJ's Deluxe—a safe distance away from the diner and home of what was arguably the best burger in all of Bronco. She hadn't considered that the restaurant was usually packed with customers. But as Sullivan had noted, it was early for lunch, so she asked Siri to call the restaurant, and breathed a sigh of relief when the hostess told her that there was a table available for 11:15 a.m.

Sullivan's truck pulled into the parking lot right behind her vehicle, and they walked into DJ's together. The high ceilings and open rafters gave the restaurant a spacious feel, while the dark wood and rich leather added a touch of elegance. The air was filled with the delicious scents of grilled meat and tangy barbecue sauce, making Sadie's empty stomach rumble.

Apparently loudly, because Sullivan looked at her, a smile tugging at the corners of his mouth.

"It sounds like somebody skipped breakfast this morning," he said.

"Not on purpose," she told him. "I had a project I wanted to finish before heading to the cemetery, and I simply forgot to eat."

The hostess led them to a narrow booth by the windows that looked out toward the mountains. When they were seated, she handed them each a leather folio and set a drink menu on the table.

Sadie glanced around at the nearby tables, where couples sat with their heads close together or their hands linked. Another booth was occupied by a dad and mom with two kids, all dressed in their Sunday best—probably stopping for brunch on their way home from church. A trio of older women sat around a square table. She recognized Fiona Nicholls—a regular customer of Holiday House—and suspected, based on an unmistakable family resemblance, that her dining companions were her sisters. But aside from the young family and the older women, almost every other table was occupied by a couple.

It shouldn't have been a revelation to Sadie, as DJ's was the most coveted spot in town for a delicious and romantic meal. But she suddenly found herself wishing that she'd suggested a different restaurant. Any other restaurant.

Because being here with Sullivan suddenly felt like a date.

Even if she knew that it wasn't.

If anything, it was an interrogation, though one that Sadie had willingly subjected herself to.

She glanced across the table. Now that the shock of his existence had worn off, she could see that while he and Bobby did look a lot alike, they weren't identical twins. Her sister's ex-husband hadn't been quite as tall or as broad across the shoulders as his brother. Also, Bobby's eyes had been more hazel than brown, his brown hair just a shade lighter, his jaw a little less square.

Another difference was that Bobby had always been quick to smile while Sullivan, at least on the two occasions that Sadie's path had crossed with his thus far, seemed noticeably less so. But there were crinkles around the corners of his eyes and laugh lines around his mouth that suggested he hadn't always been as serious as he was now. (Of course, he'd come to town to learn about his dead brother—not exactly a cause for celebration—so maybe she should cut him some slack.)

And while she'd always thought that Bobby was handsome, Sullivan was even more so. At least, in her opinion. Because she'd never felt a flutter low in her belly when she was around her former brother-in-law like she did when she was near his brother.

"I think we might have raised a few eyebrows walking in here together," Sullivan remarked.

She immediately shifted her attention back to him. "If eyebrows were raised, it's entirely *your* doing."

"Because I look so much like Bobby?"

"And because nobody—not even Bobby—knew that he had a twin brother."

"Did he grow up with any siblings?" he asked.

She shook her head. "As far as he knew, he was an only child."

"That's what I believed, too," he remarked. "At least until earlier this year."

She was curious about Sullivan's background—the parents who'd adopted him, the town where he'd grown up, the people who were his friends. She had so many questions that she wanted to ask, but she held them in check, reminding herself that they were here so that she could answer his queries.

Their server introduced herself as Lorelei as she filled their water glasses, then she recited the daily specials and asked if they wanted something from the drink menu. Although the restaurant offered an extensive list of wines and craft beers, with several pages of specialty cocktails, Sullivan opted for coffee and Sadie ordered a diet Coke. Lorelei promised to be right back with their beverages and to take their food orders.

"The service is usually prompt, so you might want to take a look at the menu before she returns," Sadie suggested when Lorelei had gone.

He obediently opened the folder. "Aren't you going to look at your menu?"

"No need," she told him. "I always order the same thing when I come here for lunch."

Which wasn't all that often, because DJ's wasn't only a little out of the way for a woman who lived and worked in Bronco Valley, it was more than a little out of her budget.

But she didn't regret that she'd brought Sullivan here today. Partly because she knew the burger she craved would likely be her lunch *and* dinner, and partly because it was his birthday—a cause for celebration even if she knew that he was also mourning his brother.

"Have you decided what you'd like?" Lorelei asked when she'd delivered their drinks.

"I'll have the barbecue bacon cheeseburger, no crispy onions, with sweet potato fries," Sadie said.

The server jotted down her requests, then shifted her attention to Sullivan. "And for you, sir?"

"That barbecue bacon cheeseburger sounds good," he decided, dumping two packets of sugar into his mug. "But I want the crispy onions and regular fries."

"I'll get your order into the kitchen right away," Lorelei promised.

Sadie picked up her soda as Sullivan stirred his coffee.

Now that they were alone again, she prepared herself for an onslaught of questions.

She wasn't prepared for him to ask, "Are you married?"

She sucked in a breath—and a mouthful of soda.

"I know it's not really any of my business," he said, as she coughed and sputtered. "And I can see there's no ring on your finger, but I wanted to be sure there isn't a jealous husband who might come after me for having lunch with his wife."

"If I had a jealous husband, I wouldn't have invited you to have lunch with me," she finally managed to respond.

"Boyfriend?" he pressed.

She shook her head. "Not jealous or otherwise."

"That's good," he said.

"Obviously your opinion differs from that of my mother," she remarked dryly. "She views my perennial single status as a character flaw—and never more so than when she's had coffee with a friend who pulls out her phone to scroll through hundreds of pictures of her grandchildren." Sadie waved a hand dismissively, embarrassed by the truth she'd spontaneously blurted out. "But you don't want to hear about that."

"Actually, I find I am intrigued by your—" he made air quotes "—perennial single status."

Sadie took another sip of her cola. "It's not a big mystery."

"So what's the explanation? Is there a shortage of single men in Bronco?"

"Hardly. But I was always Dana Chamberlin's little—and less interesting—sister. That's not to say that I haven't had relationships," she hastened to clarify. "But none of them worked out."

She breathed a silent sigh of relief when Lorelei returned with their meals, because performing a postmortem on her failed romances was *not* her idea of a good time.

Sadie plucked a sweet potato fry from her plate and dipped it in the sriracha mayo that came on the side. "Anyway, you wanted to know about the relationship between your brother and my sister, not my lack of one."

Her lunch companion was quiet for a minute, considering what she'd said. Or maybe he was contemplating how to tackle his burger.

"If you don't mind talking about it," he finally said.

"I don't mind," she said, nibbling on the fry. "I don't often get a chance to reminisce about the good parts of my sister's life."

"Their marriage was a good part?"

She heard the skepticism in his tone and understood it.

Because if Dana and Bobby's marriage had been good—why had they ended up divorced?

"Bobby was a good part," Sadie clarified. "Their marriage, like any relationship, had its ups and downs." She wiped her fingers on her napkin. "Maybe I should start at the beginning."

"That probably makes the most sense," he agreed. "But why don't you start at the beginning *after* you eat, so your food doesn't get cold?"

She nodded. "Good idea."

So they dug into their meals, chatting about inconsequential topics such as the recent weather—cold and snowy—and local holiday events—including the Christmas Tree lighting that had taken place the night before. Sadie had been there, of course; Sullivan had not, confiding that he wasn't really feeling the holiday spirit this season.

"I can understand that you wouldn't be in a celebratory mood," she said. "But I still think it's sad."

"Sad?" he echoed.

"Christmas has always been my favorite time of year," she confided. "And I can't imagine my spirits not being lifted by the twinkling lights on window displays or the oversized nutcrackers that stand sentry at town hall. As a little girl, I couldn't sleep the night before Christmas in anticipation of Santa's visit."

"Because of the mountain of presents you knew he'd leave under your tree?"

"There was never a mountain of presents under our tree. Money was tight in our house, and we knew it. But there was always at least one gift from Santa—sometimes two."

And yet, despite the fact that she'd never received

the abundance of gifts that her classmates had boasted about, there had always been something about the season that filled her heart with joy and peace. She was sorry that the man seated across from her wasn't feeling any of that—and wondering if there was any way she could help him embrace the holiday spirit.

But for now, Sadie pushed her mostly empty plate aside and returned to the subject that she knew was of most interest to her luncheon companion.

"I'll start at the beginning," she said. "The first time I met Bobby—the first time Dana brought him home to meet my mom and me—it was immediately apparent that he was head-over-heels for my sister.

"He wasn't the first. Dana had always been stunningly beautiful, and she was accustomed to guys clamoring for her attention. But none of the guys she dated seemed to hold her attention for any length of time. Not until Bobby."

"How did they meet?" Sullivan asked.

"They went to the same high school, though they ran with different crowds then, so their paths didn't really cross until Dana took a car she wanted to buy to Axle's Auto Repair for a once-over. Bobby was the mechanic who did the inspection, and he told her not to buy it, warning that it would cost her more in repairs in the first six months than the sale price.

"She bought it, anyway," Sadie told him. "But Bobby was right—the car needed a lot of work. And every time something went wrong, she took it back to Axle's, insisting that Bobby be the one to work on it.

"After her third return trip to the garage, she pointed

out that he had her phone number on the work order and demanded to know why he hadn't used it. He reminded her that he'd used it every time she'd been into the shop—to let her know when her car was ready. But he took the hint and called her again later that night, inviting her to meet him for a drink.

"It was rare for Dana to bring a boyfriend home—probably because she knew our mother wouldn't have approved of most of the guys she dated. But Bobby was different. He was kind and funny. Always quick to smile and ready to laugh, though you could tell there was so much more beneath the surface.

"Hidden depths, my mother would say. Maybe hidden demons." Sadie trailed a fingertip through the condensation on the outside of her glass. "My sister had those, too."

"Depths or demons?" Sullivan wondered aloud.

"Both," she confided.

"What was your first impression of Bobby?"

She felt her lips curve a little as she recalled that initial meeting. "That he was a genuinely nice guy. And that he could be good for my sister—if she let him.

"My mother liked him, too," she continued. "Though she cautioned me about getting attached, because Dana never hung on to any of her boyfriends for very long.

"Sure enough, they broke up. A few months later, they got back together, and then they broke up again."

"Do you know what caused the friction in their relationship?" he asked.

"Only what my sister told me—which was that it was always Bobby's fault. But despite the blow-ups, they could never stay away from one another for very long, and when they finally realized exactly that, they decided to get married.

"I worried that their relationship wasn't healthy, but there was no denying that it was passionate."

She'd painted a pretty complete portrait of Bobby and Dana's relationship, Sullivan thought, but he still had one very big question. "So how did they end up divorced?"

A shadow of something passed over her eyes—grief or maybe regret—before Sadie dropped her gaze to the table.

"Dana liked to have a good time, but she didn't know how to have a good time without a drink in her hand." She stabbed at the ice cubes in her glass with her straw. "And, over the years, she needed more and more drinks to let loose and feel good. Too many drinks."

She paused for a moment and, though her attention remained focused on the glass, he could see the sheen of tears in her eyes.

"She was an alcoholic." Sadie blew out a shaky breath. "It took me a long time to learn to say it like that—a simple fact without excuses. My sister was an alcoholic.

"It's something that Bobby and I worked on together," she confided. "When we finally recognized the truth. That she was out of control. Even then, Dana refused to see it. She insisted that she could stop drinking anytime she wanted—but why would she want to stop when she was having so much fun?"

Lorelei, interpreting Sadie's attack on the ice cubes

as a hint that her glass was empty, replaced it with a new one.

Sadie managed to smile her thanks.

"So Bobby decided it was time for some tough love," she continued when the server had gone. "And he gave her an ultimatum—him or the booze."

"She chose the booze," he guessed.

She nodded. "He was devastated—but somehow still hopeful, too. Certain that she loved him too much to risk losing him. He filed the papers, convinced that she would change her mind—and her behavior—when she realized he wasn't bluffing."

Sadie took a long sip of her soda. "But as soon as Dana was served with the petition for divorce—which she interpreted as a sign that Bobby was done with her—she went out of her way to make it clear that she was done with him, too.

"She started going out with other men. Flaunting her relationships with other men. And Bobby…he took the rejection hard."

"Even though he was the one who filed for divorce?"

"Everyone knew he didn't really want the divorce—he just wanted Dana to stop drinking so that they could start a family. Her acceptance of the end of their marriage was, in his eyes, a rejection of him and everything they'd meant to one another."

Sadie swallowed another mouthful of soda. "There are some people who blame the haunted barstool at Doug's for Bobby's death, because he was there a few days before he died, perhaps deliberately tempting fate by choosing to sit in the supposedly cursed seat. But I think, if you're looking to assign blame for what happened to your brother, you don't have to look any further than my sister."

Chapter Three

"I truly believe his fall was an accident," Sadie hastened to assure Sullivan. "But I also believe it was an accident that wouldn't have happened if he'd been paying closer attention to where he was walking, and I suspect he wasn't paying attention because he was thinking of Dana—of everything they'd had and lost."

"Do you think he might have been...more than distracted?" he ventured to ask.

"What do you mean?" she asked warily.

He hesitated, not certain he wanted an answer to the question that had been niggling at the back of his mind, but unable to hold back from asking it. "Is it possible that he was...depressed?"

"I... I don't know." She swiped at an errant tear that dropped onto her cheek. "And that's something I have to live with—because I should have known. I should have checked in with him more regularly, done something to help, so that he didn't feel alone.

"But… Dana never really liked the fact that me and Bobby were friends," she confided. "She liked it even less after the divorce, and she told me that I had to pick a side—and if I sided with Bobby, then we were no longer sisters."

Of course, she picked her sister.

How could she choose otherwise?

Sullivan hadn't even known his brother, but he had no doubt that, if tested, his loyalty would have been with the man who shared his DNA.

"I still saw him occasionally in town. At the grocery store or the diner. And I continued to take my vehicle to Axle's for maintenance. And every time I saw him, he'd give me a smile, as if he was sincerely happy to see me.

"I was glad for that. Relieved that he didn't seem to harbor any hard feelings against me for taking Dana's side. And we'd chat for a few minutes, casual conversation that seemed to be about nothing in particular, yet somehow he always managed to circle around so that he could ask about Dana. Because even after their divorce was finalized, he didn't stop loving her."

Which was the same thing that all of Bobby's drinking buddies had said, though Sadie had filled in a lot more details for him.

"Thank you for sharing all of this with me," he said, sincerely grateful to her.

"I hope it helps, at least a little, to put together a more complete picture of the man who was your brother."

"It helps a lot."

"He wasn't perfect, by any stretch of the imagination, but he was a good man. Thoughtful. Kind. Loyal." She sighed. "Unfortunately, the same words aren't ones that readily come to mind when I think about my sister."

But then she forced a smile. "And that ends our melancholy portion of the lunch hour."

"What comes next?" he asked, happy to follow her lead.

"For me, it's a bathroom break," she said. "Thanks to the three sodas I drank."

Sullivan chuckled at that as she slid out of the booth and made her way to the back of the restaurant.

He glanced at his watch again. It was just after noon, but he didn't know how much setup she might have to do prior to opening the shop. And though he was admittedly a little disappointed that their lunch date was coming to an end, he was grateful that she'd given him the time—and some valuable insights about his brother.

When Sadie came back, her eyes were sparkling again. Obviously she'd shaken off her earlier sadness and was in brighter spirits, and he was glad—because Sadie's happiness was almost infectious.

"I guess you need to get going soon," he remarked, as she slid into the seat across from him again.

"In a few minutes," she confirmed.

Their server returned to their table, this time carrying a plate with a thick wedge of chocolate cake with a lighted candle in it.

"Happy birthday," Lorelei said, as she set the plate in front of Sullivan.

He swallowed, surprised and unexpectedly touched by the thoughtful gesture. "Thank you."

As the server stepped away, Sadie smiled and said, "Now make a wish and blow out the candle."

A few weeks ago, Sullivan would have wished to know what really happened to his brother. And though that was one question Sadie hadn't been able to answer for him, sitting across from her now, he found himself wishing for the opportunity to know her better.

He blew out the candle.

She smiled again, and he felt a tug of something inside him. Because when she smiled, it was more than just a curving of her lips. Her eyes sparkled and her whole face brightened—and he was suddenly struck by the realization that she wasn't only a link to the brother he'd never known, she was also an incredibly beautiful woman.

"Lorelei offered to round up all the staff to sing to you, but I don't know you well enough to know whether that's the kind of thing you'd love or hate, so I opted for just the cake."

"I don't mind the song." In fact, he had a lot of fond memories of his mom and dad singing it to him at every birthday for as far back as he could remember. "But I'm glad you skipped it. And I'm grateful for the cake. It was a really nice gesture." He dipped his fork into the dessert, sampled the offering, and rolled his eyes heavenward. "And this is *really* good cake."

"I would expect nothing less from DJ's," she said.

"You have to try it," he said, nudging the plate toward her.

She held up her hands. "It's not my birthday."

"Don't you like chocolate cake?"

"Who doesn't like chocolate cake?"

"Well, Lorelei brought two forks," he pointed out.

She finally picked up the second fork and jabbed it into the cake. "Ohmygod," she said, speaking around a mouthful of chocolatey deliciousness. "This *is* really good cake."

"Told you." His tone was smug.

"So why are you sharing it?" she wondered. "Because if this was *my* cake, I would have picked up the extra fork and used it as a weapon against anyone who tried to steal a single crumb."

He chuckled. "You have a violent streak, do you?"

"Apparently, I do," she agreed.

"Is it okay if I have some more of my cake?" he asked. "Or am I in danger of being forked if I reach toward the plate?"

"You're safe," she assured him. "After all, I ordered it for you."

"And I'm more than happy to share it."

As he would have shared all of his birthday cakes over the years if he'd grown up with his twin brother.

But he wasn't going to let himself think about that now. Because Sadie was right—today should be a day of celebration. And yes, it sucked that Bobby wasn't around to celebrate with him, but Sullivan was pleased to know that his brother had been remembered on his birthday—and not only by him.

After another bite of cake, Sadie set her fork on the plate and picked up her phone to check the time displayed on the screen.

"And now I really have to go," she said regretfully.

He knew that she did, but he wished she didn't have to.

Because, after only a couple of hours with Sadie, he wanted more time with her. Because there was something about his brother's former sister-in-law that made the heaviness that weighed on his heart feel a little bit lighter.

"Go on, then," he said. "I'll take care of the bill."

"It's already taken care of," she told him.

"You didn't have to do that."

She responded to his protest with another smile. "I wanted to."

"Well, thank you," he said, as she slid out of the bench seat across from him. "For remembering Bobby today and sharing your memories and for lunch and…everything."

"You're welcome." She paused then, at his side of the table, and dropped a quick kiss on his cheek. "Happy birthday, Sullivan."

And then she was gone, leaving him alone with the certainty that Sadie Chamberlin was the sweetest thing he'd encountered in all his time in Bronco—and that was even after consuming a wedge of chocolate cake that could put a man in a sugar coma.

Sadie hated being late.

She was one of those people who usually headed out to her destination fifteen minutes earlier than was necessary to ensure that she wasn't tardy. Except today, when she'd stayed at the restaurant—with Sullivan—longer than she should have, and now she was running behind schedule.

The bigger surprise was that she didn't feel the least bit guilty. She wasn't even worried that there might be customers waiting outside the store when she arrived. Because while she loved selling decorations to add a festive touch to someone's home and helping shoppers find the perfect gift for someone special, neither of those things was as important as being there for a man grieving the loss of the twin brother he'd never known and having to celebrate their shared birthday on his own.

Thankfully, she had two part-time employees—Beth and Lynda—who worked for her year-round so that she didn't have to be at the shop every hour of every day. And though it was practically unheard of for Sadie not to be there to open, each of the women had a set of keys so that they could open or close, if required.

As Sadie slipped in through the back door at 1:10 p.m., she heard customers milling about in the shop, proof that Beth had, indeed, opened up on time.

It was a few hours later before the hustle and bustle quieted down and they were able to discuss anything aside from customer queries or inventory issues. And while the steady stream of shoppers meant that Sadie was far too busy to waste any time daydreaming, she nevertheless found her thoughts drifting back to Sullivan Grainger—and his questions about Bobby Stone.

Sadie had always had a soft spot for her former

brother-in-law, and she couldn't help but wonder if Sullivan's resemblance to Bobby was the reason that she'd taken an immediate liking to the newcomer—once she'd gotten over her initial shock at his appearance, anyway. Whatever the reason, spending time with him had stirred feelings inside her that hadn't been stirred in a very long time.

Beth passed a bag across the counter. "Merry Christmas."

"Merry Christmas," the happy customer echoed.

"You were late today," Beth said to Sadie when they were finally alone.

"I'm sorry." The apology was automatic but not insincere. Because, while Sadie didn't feel guilty about her tardiness, she did regret it.

"You're the boss—you don't have to apologize to me," her friend and employee responded. "I was just... surprised. I've worked here for almost six years now, and I've never known you to be late."

"Hopefully it will be another six years before it happens again," Sadie said lightly.

"I sincerely hope *not*," Beth told her. "I've said more than once that you need a life outside of the shop, and the fact that you were late gives me hope that you were doing something that might matter more to you than this business."

"I had some errands to run this morning," Sadie said.

And it was true. But then she'd crossed paths with Sullivan—and had lunch with Sullivan.

"That's not the smile of a woman who ran errands all morning," Beth noted smugly.

Sadie felt her cheeks flush, because—*darn it*—thinking about the man had caused her lips to curve. Even conscious of the fact now, she couldn't seem to stop smiling.

Instead, she busied herself tidying a display of festive snow globes. "I didn't say I ran errands *all* morning." She turned the globe in her hand and braced herself for her friend's follow-up questions as she watched the snow flutter down around a Santa figure climbing into a chimney.

But the other woman only chuckled and said, "Well, good for you."

"You're not going to press for more details?" Sadie asked warily.

"Not because I'm not curious—because I most certainly am," Beth told her. "But because I know you'll tell me when you're ready."

"Thank you," she said. "And thanks for opening up the store today."

"I didn't really have a choice," her friend confided. "At twelve fifty-nine, Carissa Howard had her face pressed against the window, trying to peer in, so I unlocked the door to save the glass from more nose prints."

"And I'll bet, after being so eager to get inside, she didn't even purchase anything." The woman was notorious for browsing and not buying.

"I don't think she planned to, but then she saw Lorraine McKenna pick up four of those melting snowman kits. I asked Lorraine why she wanted so many, and she said 'one for each of my grandchildren,' which I assured her was a fabulous idea, and then Carissa decided that she had to do the same." Beth winked. "And Carissa has seven grandkids."

Sadie chuckled. "Do we have any of those kits left?"

"Only three."

"I think it's lucky for me that you don't work on commission, or I'd have to pay you a lot more than I do now."

"You let me sell my cards in the shop, which adds a nice little bonus to my paycheck every week," Beth noted.

Of course, they both knew that Beth was the one doing Sadie the favor by providing the store with a supply of beautiful, hand-crafted greeting cards that were extremely popular with customers.

"Speaking of which—did you see the note on the bulletin board in the kitchenette?" Sadie asked.

"The one from Talia Pereira asking for fifteen unique Hanukkah cards by the tenth?"

"That's the one," she confirmed.

"I saw it—and I called Talia to tell her that I'd make them. And since things are quiet in here right now, would you mind if I took ten minutes to make a quick trip to Crafty Corner to pick up some cardstock?"

"I don't mind, but you're kidding yourself if you think you can be in and out of there in ten minutes."

"I know exactly what I need, and I promise not to get caught up looking at anything else."

"Here's a better idea," Sadie said. "Why don't you

take whatever time you need at the craft store, then head home and get started on your cards?"

"Are you sure you don't mind?"

"It's a Sunday afternoon—I think I can handle the few customers that are likely to wander in."

"It would be helpful if I could get my designs sketched out today," Beth told her.

"Then go on," Sadie urged.

"I will. And I'll see you again at noon tomorrow."

"I'll be here."

"Assuming you don't have any…errands," Beth said, with an exaggerated wink.

Sadie wished she could blame her friend's parting remark for the fact that she was thinking about Sullivan again, but the truth was, she hadn't stopped thinking about him all day.

Sullivan had just arrived back at the motel when his cell phone rang. He sighed when he saw "Mom & Dad" on the display.

It was the fourth time they'd reached out today, and he'd already let the first three calls go to voice mail. Though he wasn't in the mood to talk to them any more now than he'd been earlier, he knew they wouldn't stop calling until he answered. And while he might still be angry with them, he didn't want to cause them worry, so he swiped to connect the call.

"Hello."

"Oh." Ellie sounded startled, as if she'd been expecting his voice mail again. "Hi. Happy birthday."

"Thank you." He winced at the stiffness of his own

voice, but their relationship had changed in recent months and he didn't know how to get things back to the way they used to be—or even if he wanted to.

"Is it too much to hope that you might be home for dinner tonight?" she asked. "I've got a roast in the oven, and I baked a cake—your favorite, chocolate with—"

"I'm not going to be there for dinner." He interjected to cut her off, because he hated the plaintive tone in her voice. Hated that hearing the tone made him felt guilty about the fact that he hadn't seen Lou and Ellie in more than five months, and now his mom—*adoptive mom*—was practically begging for some of his time and attention. Time and attention that, prior to the bombshell revelation about his adoption, he'd always been more than happy to share with her.

"Maybe next weekend?" she suggested. "I can put the cake in the freezer until—"

"Probably not next weekend, either," he said, interrupting her again.

"*Probably not* means *possibly yes*," she noted hopefully.

"But more likely *no*," he told her, then added, "I'm sorry."

And he *was* sorry.

Sorry that their relationship was suddenly awkward and unfamiliar, that the two people he'd once felt closer to than anyone else in the world were strangers to him now.

"Don't apologize to me," she said, her voice breaking a little. "Please."

He was silent, not knowing what else to say.

"We'll put the cake in the freezer until the next time you're home," she decided.

"I don't know when that's going to be," he cautioned.

"You'll come home when you're ready."

Sullivan wasn't nearly as confident as Ellie sounded. He wasn't even sure what *home* was anymore.

And while he would be forever grateful to Lou and Ellie for everything they'd given him, he was still struggling to forgive them for what he felt they'd taken away—the chance to know his brother.

Chapter Four

"I didn't expect to see you again today," Sadie said when Sullivan entered Holiday House just before five o'clock, her usual closing time on Sundays.

"Is it okay that I came by?" he asked.

"Of course." Because although she was surprised by his appearance, she wasn't at all displeased—except maybe about the fact that her heart had skipped a beat when he'd walked through the door and was now pounding a little too fast for her liking.

She recognized the signs of physical attraction and wasn't comfortable realizing that she could be attracted to her former brother-in-law's twin. Or maybe it wasn't a physical attraction at all. Maybe it was simply that he looked so much like Bobby, and she still missed Bobby. Maybe her heart was simply transferring her innocent, sisterly affection for Bobby to Sullivan. Certainly, that made more sense, and the rationale eased her discomfort a little, though her heart continued to beat a little too fast.

He glanced around the empty shop. "Are you on your own?"

She nodded. "Beth was here for most of the day, but Sunday afternoons are usually pretty quiet, so she left around four." She finished folding a holiday throw and added it to the pile on display.

"I imagine every afternoon is pretty quiet in July."

She chuckled. "You'd be surprised. Not that I sell a lot of Christmas ornaments in July, but the stars-and-stripes decorations fly off the shelves."

"So you're not just a Christmas store?"

"Not even in December," she said. "Obviously, Christmas is the primary focus, but I have areas dedicated to Hanukkah and Kwanzaa, and on the second level, the rooms are filled with everything needed to celebrate New Year's, Valentine's Day, St. Patrick's Day, Easter, the Fourth of July, Diwali, Halloween and Thanksgiving. Plus we always have a selection of party decorations for birthdays, anniversaries and bridal and baby showers."

"How did you come up with the idea for Sadie's Holiday House?" he asked curiously.

"It wasn't my idea," she told him. "But it is the culmination of my dreams."

"Sounds like there's a story there," he mused.

"Not one you're likely to find interesting," she said

dismissively, as she straightened a precarious stack of boxed ornaments.

"Why don't you let me be the judge of that?" he suggested.

"You really want to know?" she asked skeptically.

"I really want to know."

She shrugged. "Holiday House originally belonged to the McCormick family. It was Victoria McCormick who started selling handmade crafts to help pay the bills when her husband was in Vietnam. When Christmas came around, she shifted her focus to holiday crafts—knitted stockings, painted baubles, rag dolls and wooden trains—and invited friends and neighbors into the front parlor where she'd put her crafts on display. They bought everything she'd made—and asked for more.

"Twenty years later, Victoria's eldest son and daughter-in-law moved their family out of this house and transformed it into a full-time retail space. Unfortunately, none of their children was interested in carrying on the business, so it passed to a niece.

"Gwendolyn McCormick, every bit as creative and talented as her grandmother, really put Holiday House on the map as *the* destination in Bronco for quality, handcrafted home décor and gifts. I met Gwen at a craft show, where I was selling Christmas wreaths, and she immediately offered to take my leftover stock on consignment.

"When I came in to drop off the wreaths—along with some tabletop centerpieces I thought she might be interested in—Gwen was swamped with holiday shoppers, so I pitched in to help. She was so grateful, she ended up offering me a part-time job for the holiday season, which eventually led to a part-time job year-round and us becoming good friends. When Gwen got sick…" Sadie paused to swallow the lump that had risen in her throat. "She asked if I'd be willing to take on more responsibility at the store so that she could keep it open.

"Naturally, I said yes, but I never expected… I didn't know that Gwen had put me on the title of the property, leaving me what had been her family's home for generations as well as the business her grandmother started."

"I'd say she made a smart choice," Sullivan said.

She managed a smile. "I like to think so."

Certainly, she'd done her best to prove—if only to herself—that she was worthy of the tremendous opportunity she'd been given. She'd poured her heart and soul into Holiday House, adding her name to the title and ultimately making it even more successful.

Spotting a blown-glass ornament in a bin of plush snowmen, she made her way across the floor to rescue the decoration and return it to its rightful place.

"But I'm sure you didn't come here for the history of my shop," she said to Sullivan now, "so why don't you tell me what brought you by?"

"I wanted to offer to make dinner for you."

She bobbled the fragile glass, exhaling a quiet sigh of relief when she'd safely set it back on the shelf.

"You want to make dinner for me?" she asked, certain she hadn't heard him correctly.

"If you don't have any other plans."

"I don't."

Unless microwaving one of the single-serve meals in her freezer and eating it while watching a holiday movie counted as plans. And even if it did, his offer was much more appealing.

"And I can't believe I'm saying this, because the idea of a home-cooked meal that I don't have to cook is wonderful, but there are other people in town who knew Bobby, maybe even better than I did," she said. "If you want a more rounded picture of your brother, you should talk to some of them."

"I've talked to quite a few of them," he assured her. "But none of them is as pretty as you."

She felt her cheeks grow warm. Though she knew she wasn't *un*attractive, Dana's radiant beauty had always cast quite a shadow over her younger, plainer sister, and Sadie was unaccustomed to men flattering her.

"Perhaps you haven't been talking to the right people," she said lightly.

"Or maybe I'd just rather hang out with you," he countered. "Unless you're uncomfortable inviting a virtual stranger into your home—even if it is to use your kitchen?"

"I'm not," she said. "Maybe I should be, but you're Bobby's brother, so I feel like I know you."

"And yet I'm still sensing some hesitation," he noted.

"Because I don't know a lot of guys who can cook," she confided. "Aside from sliding a frozen pizza into the oven, that is."

"I do a pretty good job with a frozen pizza," he told her. "But I also enjoy mixing it up every now and then."

"What do you plan on mixing up tonight?"

"What do you like?"

"Almost anything I don't have to cook," she said.

"In that case, why don't I pop over to the grocery store and meet you back here in thirty minutes?"

"Actually, I'm almost ready to close up, so you can head directly over to my place after you've done your shopping."

"That works," he said.

She scribbled her address on a sticky note for Sullivan and was just about to lock the door after him when Everlee Roberts—soon-to-be Mrs. Weston Abernathy—appeared, looking frazzled.

"Tell me you didn't sell out of those melting snowmen," Evy pleaded.

"Are you referring to the ones that you said were a horrible stocking stuffer idea?"

Her friend, the proprietor of the adjacent Cimarron Rose boutique, huffed out a breath. "I know what I said. And I still worry that some kids might feel traumatized watching their cute snowman creation melt before their eyes, but apparently my kid isn't one of them."

Sadie chuckled, thinking of her friend's adorable and precocious four-year-old daughter. "Lola did seem to be entertained by it when she was in with her Pop-Pop last week."

"But she didn't mention it to me until brunch today. Actually, she didn't mention it to *me* at all," Evy confided. "But she couldn't stop talking to Wes about it."

"And now you've realized that she'd love to find one in her stocking Christmas morning?" Sadie guessed.

"Do you have any left?" Evy asked.

She feigned regret. "We sold out today…"

Her friend's hopeful expression faded.

"…*except* for the one that I tucked away, just in case you changed your mind."

"You. Are. The. Best." Evy caught Sadie in a quick hug. "Ten percent off anything you want the next time you come into Cimarron Rose."

The boutique was a little bit boho and a whole lot cowgirl with a few unexpectedly elegant offerings, and Sadie never failed to find something she wanted to add to her wardrobe when she walked through the door. Thankfully, she was a woman who knew how to live within her means and so usually managed to restrain herself.

"I have been eyeing one of the skirts in your front window," she confessed. And a ten percent discount would help her fit the purchase into her budget. "The dark blue one with the little flowers all over it and the ruffled hem."

"It would look great on you," her friend said confidently. "We can go next door right now, if you want to try it on."

"Actually—" she glanced at her watch "—I need to get home."

"Hot date tonight?" Evy teased.

"Of course not," she immediately denied, though the heat that filled her cheeks told a different story.

"Ohmygod—you *do* have a date. And I really didn't mean to sound so surprised, but for as long as I've known you—which has admittedly only been five months—I've never known you to go out with anyone."

"And I'm not going out with anyone tonight," Sadie said. "I'm just having dinner with…a friend…at my place."

"A male friend," Evy guessed.

She rolled her eyes. "I'll see you tomorrow, Evy."

"I'm going to want details," her friend promised. "And that snowman. Bring it over when you come for the skirt."

Sullivan, his arms full of grocery bags, jabbed at the doorbell with his elbow. *Again*.

He might have worried that he was at the wrong house—that perhaps he'd misread one of the numbers on the note Sadie had given him—but from the way the house was done up for the holidays, with a fully-decorated tree visible through the front window, he felt certain that he was at the right place.

But where was Sadie?

"I'm here," she said, answering his unspoken question as she hurried up the steps behind him, her key in hand. "Sorry, a friend stopped by the shop just as I was closing up."

"No worries," he said.

She unlocked the door and pushed it open, then took one of the bags from him. "How many people are you planning on feeding?"

"You tell me," he said. "How many people live here?"

"Just me. And Elvis Presley."

He paused on the threshold. "Um… Elvis is dead," he said cautiously.

She smiled. "Only the human Elvis. The feline Elvis is very much alive and rockin' her blue suede shoes."

Though still wary, he stepped inside and followed Sadie down the hall and into a galley kitchen at the back of the house. He caught only a glimpse of the other rooms on his way by, but all had been given the holiday treatment.

Even the kitchen was in Christmas mode—with a Santa cookie jar on the counter and dish towels embroidered with "Ho Ho Ho" and a floor mat with an image of Santa's boots sticking up out of a chimney.

She set down the bag of groceries that she'd taken from him and crouched to pet the cat that strolled over to greet her.

"This is Elvis," she told Sullivan.

It was an unusual-looking creature—mostly white with splotches of beige and gray all over. "What kind of cat is he?"

"*She*," Sadie corrected him, "is a dilute calico."

"I'm more of a dog person," he confided, setting the remaining bags on the counter. "So that doesn't mean anything to me."

"A calico is a tricolored cat, most often white with patches of orange and black."

"Like a beagle," he said.

She rolled her eyes as she scooped up the cat. "A dilute calico has diluted versions of the same colors—cream and blue instead of orange and black. And these—" she shifted the cat so he could see the distinct markings on her back paws "—are her blue suede shoes."

"They look more gray than blue to me," he said.

"They're bluish gray," she insisted.

"And that's why you named her Elvis."

"Actually, Daphne Taylor named her. Well, she's Daphne Cruise now, but she was Taylor when I adopted her from Happy Hearts Animal Sanctuary three years ago."

"She should have named her Carl Perkins. He's the one who wrote and originally recorded 'Blue Suede Shoes.'"

"I didn't know that." Sadie set the cat on the floor again, then scooped food out of a container and into a bowl on the floor. "How did you know that?"

"My mom—*adoptive* mom—is a huge music buff."

As Elvis settled into her meal, Sadie washed her hands at the sink and Sullivan began unpacking the groceries.

"What are we having for dinner?" she asked.

"Lemon ginger chicken with broccoli, carrots, red peppers and jasmine rice."

She looked impressed. "My mouth is watering already."

"Stir-fries are usually pretty quick, so you shouldn't have to wait long," he told her. "Although I probably should have asked if you have a wok."

"I have a deep frying pan."

"That'll do."

She retrieved the pan from the drawer beneath the stove.

"What else do you need?"

"A cutting board and a sharp knife. Actually, two cutting boards and knives." Because there was no way he'd chop vegetables on the same one he'd used to cut up the chicken breasts. "A pot for the rice. Measuring cups."

She gathered the items he requested.

"What can I do to help?" she asked.

"The whole point of letting someone cook dinner for you is that you don't have to do anything," he told her.

She shrugged. "I can't just sit back while someone else does the work."

"Do you want to peel carrots?" he asked.

"It's only my…sixteenth favorite thing to do in the whole world."

He chuckled and gestured to the drawers. "Well, I'm sure you can find your peeler more easily than I could."

She started peeling while he got to work on the chicken breasts.

"How many do you want peeled?" she asked, as she set the first one aside.

"Three should be good."

"Why did you buy a two-pound bag if you only needed three carrots?"

"Because the five-pound bag seemed like overkill."

She chuckled at his deadpan response. "I'm guessing that was your rationale for the two-pound bag of onions, too?"

"It was." He drizzled olive oil in the hot pan, swirled it around, then added the minced garlic and diced onion.

"I should have gone to the grocery store with you," she said. "So that you didn't waste money on items I already have in my cupboard and refrigerator."

"I didn't spend a lot of money," he told her. "Certainly less than you'd pay for a meal in a restaurant."

"I'd say that depends on the restaurant."

"Anyway, I wanted to do this for you."

"And I appreciate it," she said. "But I would have been just as happy if you'd picked up a pizza at Bronco Brick Oven."

"Maybe next time." He winced at the automatic response—at the implication that there might be a next time. Because the truth was, he wasn't sure what he was doing there now, except that he'd been feeling a little out of sorts after talking to his mom and hadn't wanted to hang out in his motel room alone.

Which was strange, because *alone* had been his status quo for the past several months. He'd been speaking nothing more than the truth when he'd said that he hadn't made any friends in Bronco.

If that's true, it's only because you haven't tried.

Sadie was right about that—he hadn't tried. He'd deliberately kept to himself, too angry with the so-called friends of Bobby's who seemed to have forgotten about him to want to get to know them.

But Sadie hadn't forgotten Bobby. Her appearance at the cemetery this morning proved that. And he thought, maybe, they'd taken a step toward becoming friends.

He'd enjoyed talking with her over lunch at DJ's. Even more significant, when he was with Sadie, he didn't feel alone. Despite the fact that he'd only met her nine days ago—and really only spent any time with her today—he felt as if there was a connection between them.

Something more than the fact that her sister had been married to his brother.

But if they were going to spend more time together, he was going to have to stop noticing how pretty she was. How her long skirt swirled around her legs as she moved. How her fuzzy sweater hugged her breasts. How her lips—quick to curve into a sunny smile— tempted a man to taste. How the pulse point at the base of her jaw seemed to beat a little bit faster when he stood close to her.

Was it possible that Sadie was attracted to him?

The idea was intriguing.

Another explanation—that her physical response was based on his likeness to his twin, that she'd been attracted to Bobby—was more than a little disconcerting.

Either way, it shouldn't matter. Because he had no interest in any kind of romantic involvement—especially not with his twin brother's former sister-in-law.

But if they could be friends…he'd be okay with that.

Not just okay, but satisfied, he decided. Because it would be foolish and futile to wish for anything more.

Chapter Five

"Do you want these sliced?" Sadie asked, gesturing to the carrots she'd peeled.

Sullivan glanced over his shoulder as he continued to push the chicken around in the pan, nodded. "That would be great—thanks."

She swapped her peeler for a knife and began cutting the carrots into thin, even rounds as he shifted his attention to the broccoli, chopping it into bite-sized florets.

This was nice, sharing kitchen duties with someone, Sadie thought. Exchanging little bits of conversation as they worked together to prepare dinner.

Even Harlow, the man she'd lived with and thought she was going to marry, hadn't offered to help with meal prep—or any of the myriad of responsibilities that were required to keep a house running smoothly. Sure, he'd change lightbulbs and tighten loose screws and take out the garbage, but he seemed happy with the traditional division of labor, never mind that she'd worked even longer hours outside of the home than he did.

To be fair, he'd sometimes offered to help with the cleanup after dinner, though not if there was a game on TV—and it seemed to Sadie that there was almost always some kind of game on TV.

But Harlow had moved out to California two years ago, and Sadie didn't miss him anymore. The truth was, he'd only been gone a few weeks when she'd realized her life hadn't changed very much in his absence. And more than she'd missed him, she'd missed the idea of sharing her life with someone. She'd missed the comfort of being in a relationship, with the anticipation of someday being a bride and then a wife and a mother.

She hadn't entirely given up hope that she might be all of those things someday, but for now, she had Elvis. She loved snuggling on the sofa with the cat at the end of the day, even if Elvis wasn't much of a conversationalist.

And maybe most men were like Harlow. The fact that Sullivan had offered to cook one meal for her didn't prove any differently.

But he did seem to know his way around the kitchen. Chopping and measuring and mixing as if he did so on a regular basis and not just on rare occasions in an effort to impress a woman.

Not that she thought he was trying to impress *her*.

More likely, he'd been feeling lonely and just wanted some company.

He added the vegetables to the pan and stirred the rice.

Since he seemed to have everything under control, she got out plates and cutlery to set the table.

She'd been certain that Sullivan had showed up at Holiday House with an offer to cook dinner because he'd wanted to talk about Bobby some more. Which she had absolutely no objection to. She could only imagine how difficult it had been for him to learn that he had a brother he'd never have a chance to know. Though Sadie and Dana hadn't been particularly close in the last years of her sister's life, she cherished the memories she had of times they'd spent together and still mourned her loss. Especially because there was no reason, aside from her own poor choices, for Dana to have died so young.

So she was surprised that Sullivan hadn't mentioned his brother's name once while he was cooking. To be honest, they hadn't talked about much of anything, but even the quiet had been nice with his company.

"I've got a bottle of Chardonnay in the fridge," she said. "Would you like a glass with dinner?"

"That sounds good."

She set wineglasses on the table.

"I just realized that you must have walked home today," Sullivan said, as he retrieved the plates to dish up the meal. "Because I would have heard a vehicle pull into the driveway when I was standing at the door."

"I did," she confirmed. "There was a delivery truck

blocking the parking lot when I left the shop, and I figured I could get home faster if I walked rather than sit in my car waiting for it to move."

He frowned. "And now you'll have to walk back in the morning."

"I prefer to walk." She poured the wine. "I only drove today because I had errands this morning and then I was running behind schedule after lunch."

"My fault," he said.

"No one's fault," she denied, taking a seat at the table. She waited for him to do the same and lifted her glass. "Thank you for this."

"It was my pleasure," he told her, clinking his glass against hers.

They each sipped the wine, then dug into the food.

After such a big lunch, Sadie didn't think she'd be hungry, but she'd worked up an appetite being on her feet all afternoon. Or maybe it was simply that the meal was so good, that her plate was nearly half empty before she paused to say, "This is…amazing."

"I'm glad you like it."

"*Like* is a serious understatement," she told him, as she stabbed another broccoli floret with her fork. "Where did you learn to cook?"

"My mom—*adoptive* mom," he quickly amended.

She took another sip of her wine. "You don't have to do that all the time, you know," she said gently.

He scooped up a forkful of rice. "Do what?"

"Clarify that your mom and your dad are your adoptive parents."

"I guess I've been doing it inside my head so often

over the past several months, to remind myself that they're not who I always believed them to be—that *I'm* not who I believed myself to be—that it's become a habit."

"But they *are* your parents," Sadie pointed out. "Just because they didn't contribute to your DNA doesn't negate the facts that they raised you, supported you, loved you."

"And lied to me." Sullivan pushed a carrot around his plate. "Even now, I wouldn't know the truth if I hadn't been digging in my parents' attic," he confided. "And that was only at the request of my aunt, who wanted to put together a scrapbook for Louis and Ellie's upcoming fiftieth wedding anniversary."

"Your parents have been married for fifty years?"

"Almost," he said. "Their anniversary is at the end of February."

"That's an impressive milestone," she noted.

"Yeah," he agreed.

Which meant that they'd been married more than ten years before they'd adopted Sullivan, perhaps having tried desperately for a child all of those years, and finally being gifted with another woman's baby.

Because any child was a gift, and Sadie imagined that was even more true for parents who adopted a child. After Harlow had moved to California, Sadie had given some thought to adoption herself, because she really wanted to be a mother. But she'd decided to put the idea on the back burner for now, not quite ready to give up hope that she might find a partner with whom to raise a child someday.

"Anyway, I found the photo albums my aunt wanted," Sullivan continued. "Along with an old and faded Certificate of Adoption."

"Is that when you confronted your parents?" she asked.

He nodded. "And when they finally admitted that I wasn't their biological child—and also that they'd never intended for me to find out the truth."

"Did they explain why?"

"They said it was because the minute the papers were signed, I became their son in every way that mattered."

"It sounds as if they love you very much."

"I know they do." He sighed. "And yet, if you really love someone, would you withhold something so crucial to their identity? And for thirty-eight years?"

"You're asking the wrong person," Sadie told him. "My father didn't love his family enough to stick around past my seventh birthday."

"I'm sorry."

She shrugged. "I'm just saying that maybe you should cut them some slack, because even if they did the wrong thing—and obviously they should have told you the truth years ago—they were motivated by love for you."

"Was it love?" he wondered. "Or was it fear?"

"What do you think they were afraid of?"

He shrugged. "Losing the child they'd taken in."

"And have they lost you?" she asked.

"Of course not."

Sadie lifted her glass, sipped her wine. "How long have you been in Bronco?"

"Five months," he admitted.

"And how many times have you been home in the past five months?"

"What does that have to do with anything?" he challenged.

She shrugged. "Maybe nothing."

"I just need time to work through some things," he said.

"Why did you decide to do that in Bronco?"

"Because this is where Bobby lived. I came here looking for information about my brother," he reminded her. "Once I got over the shock of discovering that I'd been adopted, I decided to look for my birth parents, so I had a DNA test done and uploaded the results to one of those online family trees, hoping for a match that might lead to one of my birth parents. I wasn't expecting to discover that I had a brother—a twin, I realized, when I saw that our birth dates were the same."

"That must have been quite a surprise," Sadie mused.

"You have no idea," he told her. "But once the shock wore off, I was excited and eager to reach out. A typical only child, I'd always wanted a sibling and couldn't wait to get to know mine. So, I immediately tried to learn more about him, to track him down and set up a meeting.

"What I learned was that Bobby Stone—the brother I never got to know—was dead."

"I'm so sorry."

"But I couldn't let it go. It just seemed wrong to get so close and then walk away empty-handed. I wanted—

needed—to know what really happened. That's why I came to Bronco."

"Unfortunately, the only one who really knows what happened is Bobby," Sadie reminded him gently. "But all the evidence points in the direction of a hiking accident."

"If an abandoned backpack and some broken tree branches can be called evidence," he said.

"I agree it's not a lot, but even the best investigators can't find what's not there."

"Like a body?" he guessed.

She nodded.

He hesitated a moment, reluctant to ask the question that desperately needed an answer. "Do *you* think he's dead?"

Sadie paused, too, as if unwilling to give an answer she knew he wouldn't want to hear. "I wish I could say no," she finally responded. "But the truth is, I'm sure he is. Because the Bobby I knew wouldn't have let his friends grieve and mourn if he wasn't."

"You mean he wouldn't have let *you* believe he was dead?" Sullivan guessed. "Because, as far as I can tell, you're the only one who still thinks about him, three years later."

"I'm sure I'm not the only one who thinks about him," she protested, reaching for her glass again. "But yes, I would hope, if he was alive, he would have been in touch."

"And yet, there's part of you that wonders," he said. "Otherwise, you wouldn't have assumed that I was Bobby when I showed up in your shop."

"I didn't know Bobby had a brother," she reminded him. "And the resemblance between the two of you is uncanny."

"Can I ask you another question?"

"Ask away," she urged.

"Did Bobby often go hiking alone?"

"That, I can't tell you," she said. "He and Dana used to hike together sometimes. But after their marriage fell apart... I don't know. He always loved being outdoors, and I don't imagine the divorce papers would change that. But I can't say for sure whether or not his actions that day were out of character."

He nodded and set his fork and knife on top of his empty plate.

"Now I have a question for you," Sadie said.

"What's that?" he asked.

"Why all the subterfuge?"

"I'm not sure I know what you mean," he hedged.

"You've been skulking around town for months, trying to dig up information about your brother from the shadows."

His lips twitched as he fought against a smile. "I don't know that I've ever been accused of skulking before."

"But that's what you were doing."

"Maybe," he acknowledged.

"My point is that if you'd just walked into Doug's bar on day one and explained that you were Bobby's brother, people would have been happy to answer your questions."

"So maybe I was worried that I wouldn't be able to answer *their* questions," he finally confided.

"It makes sense that they'd be just as curious about you as you are about Bobby," she noted. "So what made you decide to come out of hiding?"

"A conversation with my mom. My—" He caught himself before he could say *adoptive* again. "I ignored their calls for a long time after I left," he continued. "I didn't want to talk to them, because I couldn't forgive them for the deception they'd perpetrated about my birth for thirty-eight years. Then I realized that I was searching so hard for information about Bobby because he was my brother—my family. And while I didn't share DNA with Lou and Ellie, they are the only parents I've ever known, and I didn't want to lose them.

"So the next time my mom called, I answered. As we talked, she could tell I was frustrated that I wasn't having any luck in my search for information about my brother and suggested that, if I wanted to know about Bobby's life—and death—I needed to talk to the people who knew him."

"And that's how you ended up at Holiday House at the end of November," she guessed.

He nodded again.

"Unfortunately, we didn't have much of a chance to chat that day," she remembered.

"But we've made some good progress today," he noted.

"I think so, too," she agreed. "And because of that, I'm going to overstep the bounds of our fledgling friendship and ask if you talked to your parents today, because it's an important day for them, too."

"Actually, I did," he confided. "I think my mom was disappointed that I wasn't going to be home to celebrate with them, but she insisted that she'd put the cake she'd made for me in the freezer until I came home."

"They obviously miss you," Sadie noted.

"Yeah."

"And I bet you miss them, too."

He didn't respond to that.

"You can be angry at them and miss them, too," she said gently. "It's normal to have conflicting feelings about those we love."

"Is it?" he wondered.

"Certainly in my experience," she said. "I hated my father for leaving and, at the same time, I would have given anything for him to come home. And while I sometimes resented my sister's selfishness, she was still my best friend growing up. And my mom occasionally makes me crazy, but I always love her."

"Maybe you're right," he allowed. "I've never gone more than a few days without seeing them. Before I came to Bronco, I mean. I've been living on my own for almost fifteen years, but it wasn't unusual for me to stop by their house once or twice a week.

"Anyway, I've been thinking that, if I'm going to stay here much longer, I should look for a job."

Sadie cautioned herself against reading too much into his remark. Staying longer didn't mean staying forever, and it would be a mistake to let herself get attached to him. But she wasn't sure she could do anything about the attraction that already hummed in her veins—except ignore it, and so that's what she intended to do.

"You mentioned that you've been in Bronco for the past several months," she remarked, turning her focus back to their conversation. "But where did you come from? You left that part out."

"Columbus. Montana, not Ohio," he clarified, before she could ask.

Not so very far, she noted.

"What did you do there?"

"I worked as a wind tech."

"We don't have many wind farms in Bronco," she told him.

"But you do have ranches," he noted. "And I have some experience ranching."

She smiled. "Every little boy dreams of being a cowboy. Unfortunately, I don't know that you'll find many ranches hiring this time of year.

"Although I did hear that the Flying A might be looking for an extra hand over the holidays," she suddenly remembered, as she pushed away from the table and carried their empty plates to the counter.

"That's the Abernathy ranch, isn't it?"

"Hutch and Hannah Abernathy's ranch," she clarified. "George and Angela Abernathy's ranch is the Ambling A."

"Unfortunately, I don't think anyone named Abernathy is going to want to hire me."

"Why would you say that?"

"Because of what happened to Weston Garrett at Doug's bar in July."

"Are you talking about the rock that went through the window?"

He nodded.

Her eyes went wide. "That was *you*?"

"No!" His denial was immediate and vehement. "But I might have been *indirectly* responsible."

"I'm going to need some more details," Sadie told him.

He sighed. "You already know that I came to Bronco to learn everything I could about my brother, and I was pleased by the outpouring of support I'd found for Bobby online. But by the time I arrived in town, it seemed as if my brother had been completely forgotten by everyone who'd claimed to care so much, so…"

"So what?" Sadie pressed, when his explanation trailed off.

"So I wanted to remind them," he confided, with a regretful shake of his head. "I thought I was being clever, writing his name—Bobby Stone—on a stone."

"It might have been clever, but it was also dangerous," Sadie said, unimpressed. "Someone could have been seriously hurt when you tossed it through the window at Doug's bar."

"But I didn't toss it through the window," he protested. "By that time, I'd gotten more than a few double-takes from local residents and decided that I should lay low for a while."

"So how did the rock end up crashing through the window?" she challenged.

"I offered twenty bucks to a local high school kid to deliver it to the bar. I wanted him to put it on the haunted stool—where Bobby had supposedly sat only days before his disappearance. I guess I was just so overwhelmed by my own frustration that I wasn't thinking clearly when I came up with that plan. It didn't occur to me that the kid was afraid to go into the bar where his dad is a regular."

"You're saying he's the one who threw the rock?"

"I guess he wanted to be sure he'd earned the twenty bucks I'd paid him to deliver it."

"Someone could have been seriously hurt," Sadie said again.

"I know. And I felt horrible when I heard what happened—and relieved that there weren't any significant injuries. That's when I decided that paper was safer than rocks."

"And when you began putting up flyers around town, urging people to remember Bobby Stone?" she guessed.

Now he nodded.

"And it worked," she noted. "Because suddenly everyone was talking about Bobby again."

"Although not the way I'd hoped," he acknowledged. "Someone must have seen me with the flyers and, instead of remembering him, started a rumor that Bobby's ghost was haunting the town."

"And now Bobby's brother is going to apply for a job at the Flying A," she mused.

"I didn't say I was going to apply for the job," he pointed out.

"But you will," Sadie said confidently.

And she was hopeful that he would get it, because she was looking forward to seeing a lot more of Sullivan Grainger around town.

Chapter Six

Monday was usually the slowest day of the week at Sadie's Holiday House, but even "slowest" didn't mean "slow" in December. Not that she was complaining. The nature of her business meant there were inevitable ebbs and flows with the seasons, and Sadie relied on the busier months to sustain her through the lean ones.

But today, she had boxes of new inventory to unpack and display. She liked to showcase the work of nearby crafters and artisans as much as possible, and she'd been thrilled to discover Wick-ed, the label of a local candle-maker who created clean-burning and long-lasting vegan candles. The current shipment included pillars in festive colors decorated with miniature pinecones and holly leaves. After a selection of the candles had been set out on display, Lynda came in carrying two more boxes.

Like Beth, Lynda was more than an employee and friend—she was also a talented crafter who specialized in needle felting. This time of year, her angel tree toppers were a favorite of many customers.

"These are the special orders," Lynda said, setting one of the boxes behind the counter. "These are regular inventory." She carried the second box to the shelf and began putting them on display.

There was a steady flow of customers throughout the day—with a bit of a rush between noon and two o'clock, coinciding with the lunch breaks of others who worked in Valley Center. The shop owners on Commercial Street all supported one another and had helped spearhead the successful resurgence of the retail offerings in Bronco Valley.

Anna Rowling, who worked at Tink's Toy Box, was a regular customer and one who boasted a nutcracker collection that put the selection at Holiday House to shame. Nevertheless, she came in at the beginning of December every year, looking for something new and different. This year, she'd had a specific request, and though it had taken some searching, Sadie had finally managed to get her hands on what the woman wanted.

"What do you think?" she asked, opening the box so her customer could see the wooden figure.

Anna's eyes got misty. "It's perfect."

Sadie smiled. "I thought so, too."

The brightly colored nutcracker wasn't holding the traditional sword or rifle or even drumsticks, but a Pride flag.

"My nephew hasn't come out to his parents yet,"

Anna confided. "He hasn't officially come out to me, either, but I know—and I think he knows that I know."

"He's lucky to have you in his corner," Sadie said.

"I just want him to feel confident that I am—and that I'll always love and support him."

"This should give him the message." She returned the nutcracker to the box and closed the lid. "As well as being a beautiful addition to your collection."

Not long after Anna had gone, Roberta came in.

"I didn't expect to see you today," Sadie said, greeting her mom with a hug and a kiss.

"Things were slow at the restaurant, so Wayne offered to let me clock out early."

Sadie knew the man's "offer" had likely been more of a directive—because sending home an idle server meant fewer wages out of the Gemstone Diner owner's pocket, completely disregarding the fact that it also meant fewer tips in Roberta's. But her mom didn't have as many expenses now as she'd had when she was raising two kids. In fact, she would manage just fine with her income from her second job at a local flower shop if she gave up waiting tables at the diner, as Sadie frequently reminded her. But Roberta had been doing it for so long that she'd become friends with many of the regular customers and enjoyed the brief interactions they shared as she served them.

"Are you heading home now then?" Sadie asked.

"I am," Roberta confirmed. "But I was hoping to have a cup of tea with my daughter first, if she has a few minutes to spare."

"Her boss is known to be quite a taskmaster," Sadie

said teasingly. "But I'm sure she can sneak into the kitchen for a bit."

The shop had undergone a lot of renovations over the years to transform the former residence into a retail space. And though the kitchen had been downsized, the basic components remained, including a bistro table and two chairs.

Roberta settled into one of the chairs while Sadie filled the electric kettle from the tap, then plugged it in and selected two mugs from the cupboard.

"What kind of tea would you like?"

"As if I don't always have Earl Grey," her mom said.

"You always have Earl Grey *except* when I've got the Holiday Wishes blend."

"Is that the orange cinnamon one?" Roberta asked hopefully.

"It is."

"Then I'll have Holiday Wishes."

Sadie dropped a bag into each of the mugs. "There's a tin of shortbread cookies on the table, if you want something to nibble with your tea."

Her mom shook her head. "No, thanks. I spend far too much time sampling and nibbling this time of year."

"Don't we all?" Sadie agreed. "Actually, I haven't had my lunch yet, and I've got some leftover chicken stir-fry I could heat up for both of us to share."

"No, thanks," Roberta said again. "I had soup and a sandwich at the diner—but you go ahead and eat."

"Later," she decided, pouring hot water into the mugs and carrying them to the table.

"Thank you," Roberta murmured almost absently.

"Is everything okay?" Sadie asked.

"Yeah." Her mom added a generous spoonful of sugar to her tea. "I was looking at those tree toppers that Lynda makes, thinking I might get one to replace that old star with half the lights burned out, but I'm not sure I'll bother putting the tree up this year."

"What do you mean? It's Christmas. You can't celebrate Christmas without a tree."

"I'm pretty sure you can," Roberta said, a hint of a smile playing around the corners of her mouth. "Or maybe *you* can't, but *I* can."

"Where is this coming from?" Sadie asked, concerned. "You've always loved Christmas as much as I do."

But that wasn't really true, she realized now.

Since Dana's passing, almost three years ago, the holidays had been more bittersweet than joyful for Roberta, who preferred to reminisce about Christmases past than celebrate in the present. And while her sister's death had been a shock to Sadie, too, she'd managed to separate that devastating loss from the season.

"I'm getting older, you know," Roberta pointed out. Because she wouldn't bring up the loss of her oldest daughter, no matter that Dana's death had to be on both of their minds. "Myrtle Edmundson told me she hasn't put up a tree in more than a dozen years."

"Myrtle Edmundson celebrated her ninetieth birthday in October," Sadie pointed out to her mom. "You're only sixty-two."

"Still, it's a lot of work."

"What if I came over to help?"

"That would be nice," Roberta said. "But you're so busy this time of year. I couldn't ask that of you."

"You didn't ask, I offered," she said. "Are you working Wednesday night?"

Her mom shook her head. "I finish at three on Wednesday."

"I'm here until five, so I'll pick up pizza and head over to your place for six."

"I can make something for us for dinner," Roberta said.

"I know you can," Sadie agreed. "But I thought pizza would be a nice treat."

"It would, but I'm actually meeting some friends at Bronco Brick Oven tonight," her mom confided.

And while Sadie would never object to having pizza twice in one week, she knew that her mother would consider it an indulgence—and Roberta wasn't one to indulge.

"I'll pick up something else then," she decided.

"And I'll make sure I've got my decorations out of storage." Roberta swallowed her last mouthful of tea.

"Before you go," Sadie said, touching a hand to her mother's arm before she could push away from the table. "There's something I want to tell you."

"What is it?" Roberta asked, a furrow in her brow.

"I don't know if you'd heard any of the rumors about Bobby's ghost haunting the town—"

"You know I don't believe in ghosts," her mom said dismissively.

"I know," Sadie confirmed. "But you might have second thoughts about that if you met Sullivan Grainger."

"Who is Sullivan Grainger?"

"Bobby's twin brother."

Sadie was right, Sullivan acknowledged, as he drove toward the Flying A the following afternoon. At least about the part that he needed a job. And after an extensive search of the local paper and online classified ads had revealed that job postings were few and far between, he'd emailed a copy of his résumé to Garrett Abernathy.

Within half an hour of hitting Send, he'd received a reply inviting him to come out to the ranch for an interview.

As he got out of his truck, he saw a woman walking through the snow, a dog trotting at her heels. Though she was a fair distance away, she offered a friendly wave and he returned the gesture.

Maybe making friends in Bronco wouldn't be too difficult, if he was willing to make a little bit of effort. But he wasn't yet ready to count on adding any of the Abernathys to his Christmas card list. Not even if he had a list and actually sent cards.

Following the instructions in the email, he walked into the barn, making his way past the horses' stalls to the office at the far end. Sullivan relaxed a little as he breathed in the familiar scents of fresh hay and animals, saddle soap and leather. It had been a lot of years since he'd worked on a ranch, but he'd enjoyed the physical labor when he did and hoped he'd have the opportunity to do so again.

A brass plaque on the partially open door identified it as the office, and he knocked briskly.

"Come on in."

Inside, he discovered a nicely appointed space with lots of dark wood and leather furniture. A man he recognized from his first visit to Sadie's Holiday House pushed a chair back from the desk and rose to his feet, offering his hand.

"You're not Bobby Stone," he noted, obviously recalling the same encounter. "So you must be Sullivan Grainger."

Sullivan nodded. "It's a pleasure to meet you, Mr. Abernathy."

"Garrett, please." He gestured for Sullivan to take a seat.

He sat, and his prospective employer did the same.

"I looked at your résumé," Garrett said. "And considering your recent job experience, I'm curious to know why you're looking for work as a ranch hand."

"Because there are no wind farms in Bronco."

"Not yet, anyway," the rancher agreed.

And though that remark piqued his interest, Sullivan forced himself to stay focused on the purpose of this interview.

"We don't hire a lot of hands," Garrett continued. "We don't usually need to, because there are enough Abernathys around to handle the daily chores. But me and Brynn are going to be out of town for the next few weeks, and I know my brothers will be grateful to have some help."

"I haven't done ranch work in a few years," Sullivan admitted. "But I'm a fast learner and a hard worker."

"That's what Warren Higgins said."

Sullivan wasn't surprised that the rancher had already called his former boss. The Abernathys didn't get to be as successful as they were by taking chances and hiring unqualified people.

"So…when can you start?" Garrett asked.

Apparently, he was being offered the job.

Sullivan managed to hold back his grin. "Today," he said. "Now. Whenever you need me."

"Tomorrow would be fine," Garrett said. "Today you should pack up your stuff and check out of the motel I heard you've been staying at." He opened his desk drawer and took out a key. "You can have Cabin Three."

The job listing had indicated that lodging was included, but Sullivan hadn't expected anything more than a bunk in a room shared with a handful of other ranch hands. It was a relief to know that he'd have some privacy—and that he'd finally be able to move out of the drab room that had been his home for the past few months.

"What time do we start in the morning?"

"Six a.m."

Sullivan winced inwardly. "That's early."

"Yep," Garrett readily agreed. "Don't be late."

"I won't," he promised.

"You haven't asked about salary," his new boss noted.

"But I did want to talk to you about that," Sullivan said.

"Ranch hands are paid on the first and fifteenth

of each month. Since we're already past the first, you won't see any money until the fifteenth." Garrett passed a paper across the desk. "Fill this out and your pay will automatically be deposited into your account."

"Actually, what I wanted to talk about was maybe working without pay for the first few weeks—or however long you think is appropriate…as restitution for what happened at Doug's bar back in July."

The other man leaned back in his chair and studied him across the expanse of his desk for a long moment. "I've never had an employee want to work for free before," he finally remarked.

Sullivan resisted the urge to shift in his chair or give any other outward sign of the guilt that had been eating away at him for the past several months. "Maybe because you've never had an employee who was responsible for your brother being injured."

"Did you throw the rock through the window?"

"No," Sullivan said. "But I'm responsible, because I gave it to the kid who threw it."

"And I'm guessing you're the anonymous *someone* who paid for Doug to have the window repaired."

He cleared his throat. "It seemed the least I could do."

"Well, the way I see it, you made your restitution," Garrett said. "Wes only got hit because he was playing hero—and since he got the girl he wanted, it all worked out in the end."

"That's quite magnanimous of you."

The rancher shrugged. "I don't know a man who's

never made a mistake. The fact that you owned up to what you did proves to me that you're a stand-up guy." He stood then and offered his hand. "Welcome to the Flying A."

Chapter Seven

Evy stopped by Holiday House later that afternoon.

"You didn't come in for the skirt," she said, her gaze narrowed suspiciously.

"I didn't have a chance," Sadie told her. "My mom stopped by earlier, and from the moment she left until right now, I've barely had a moment to catch my breath."

"I thought maybe one of your employees had sold the last melting snowman."

"I wouldn't let that happen," she promised.

"Well, give me the snowman and I'll give you this," Evy said, holding up a paper bag.

"Are you seriously ransoming the skirt for the snowman?" Sadie asked, amused.

"A mom's gotta do what a mom's gotta do," her friend said.

Smiling, Sadie went behind the counter to retrieve the novelty gift that she'd set aside. "Here it is."

"And here you go."

She pulled the skirt out of the bag. "Oh, it's even prettier than I remembered." The fabric was soft and flowy, and the dark blue buttons that ran all the way down the front were shaped like flowers. She held it up to her waist, then turned it around. "Where's the price tag?"

"It must have fallen off."

"Well, how much is it?" Sadie wanted to know.

"It doesn't matter, because I'm not selling it to you," her friend said. "I'm giving it to you."

"That doesn't seem like a fair trade," she protested. "This skirt probably cost three or four—maybe even five—times as much as the snowman."

"Only because my merchandise markup is so high," Evy said.

"We both know it's not."

Her friend shrugged.

"Please let me pay you for this."

"No."

Sadie sighed.

"Okay," Evy relented. "If you want to give me something else, how about the inside scoop on your new man?"

"I don't have a new man."

"Really? Because I heard through the grapevine that you've been spending a lot of time with Sullivan Grainger," her friend remarked.

"Aren't grapevines frozen this time of year?"

"No way. The hot gossip that flows through keeps them thawed."

Sadie couldn't help but smile at her friend's quick response.

"Well, I don't know that it's accurate to say that I've been spending *a lot* of time with him—but I did cross paths with him at the cemetery yesterday, after which we had lunch together at DJ's. And then, because I bought his lunch, because it was his birthday, he offered to make dinner for me."

"I knew the friend you were having dinner with was a man," Evy said smugly. "But wait a minute… Are you telling me that he cooked for you?"

Sadie nodded.

"I'm impressed. Or maybe I'm giving him too much credit with too few details. What did he make? And was it any good?"

She chuckled. "It was a lemon ginger chicken stir-fry and it was delicious."

"Okay, so I'm impressed," Evy said again. "Then again, my heart completely melted when I found Wes in my kitchen, stirring soup and flipping sandwiches."

"I bet he could have been stirring dirty socks in a pot on the stove and you would have melted—because it was Wes."

"Maybe," her friend allowed. "Although, at the time, I swore I wasn't looking to fall in love."

"That's usually when it happens, isn't it?"

"Is that what's happening with you and Sullivan?"

"No," Sadie said, shaking her head for emphasis. "It's not like that."

"So you're not attracted to him?" her friend challenged.

"I didn't say that," she hedged.

"So you *are* attracted to him."

"He's a good-looking man," Sadie said. "Strong and handsome, with a surprisingly sensitive side."

"It sounds to me as if it's *exactly* like that," Evy noted.

"You sound like my mother," Sadie grumbled.

Her friend's brows lifted. "You told your mom about Sullivan?"

"I wasn't going to, because I know that any mention of Bobby makes her think of Dana, which inevitably makes her sad. But she was already feeling a little sad when she was here earlier, and I was worried that if I didn't say something, she'd hear about him from someone else, and I figured the news that Bobby had a twin brother would be better received coming from me."

"Was it?" Evy asked gently.

"I think so. But maybe I said too much, because she warned me against getting involved with a man who's obviously carrying a lot of baggage."

"It does sound as if he's got a lot of baggage."

"How can he not?" Sadie said. "But neither you nor my mom need to worry about me, because I'm not involved with him."

"Are you sure?" her friend pressed.

"Yes, I'm sure. You don't think I'd know if I was involved with somebody?"

Evy rolled her eyes. "What I was going to say is that everyone has baggage, and that shouldn't be a reason to disregard the possibility of a relationship with an interesting man you obviously enjoy spending time with."

"I'm not worried about his baggage," Sadie said. "But I'm also not interested in anything more than being his friend."

"Because you're afraid of history repeating itself," her friend said sympathetically.

"Maybe," she allowed.

"Definitely," Evy countered. "And that's normal. When I first started dating Wes, I had more than a few concerns that he was just like Lola's father."

"Wes is nothing like Chad," she immediately replied. Though she'd never actually met the man who'd gotten Evy pregnant, her friend had told Sadie the story, so she felt confident in her assertion.

"I know that now," Evy acknowledged. "But they were both wealthy and handsome and popular—and I just wanted to find a man of substance. Someone like my dad, who commits one hundred percent to those he loves."

"I'm definitely not looking for anyone like *my* dad," Sadie said. "Or Michael or Harlow."

Or Bobby.

Of course, she didn't say his name aloud. But she'd loved Bobby, too, though in a different way than she'd loved her father and her high school boyfriend and almost-fiancé. Because he'd been a friend and a brother, and now he was gone, too.

An alarm on Evy's phone went off. "I'm sorry, but I've gotta run to pick up Lola from daycare."

"Don't apologize," Sadie said.

"Can we finish this conversation later?"

"This conversation *is* finished." She gently took her friend by the shoulders and turned her toward the door. "You don't want to keep Lola waiting."

After Evy had gone, Sadie kept herself busy with customers and *not* thinking about what her friend had said. Because even if she was afraid of history repeating itself, she had good reason. Because every man she'd ever loved had left her, and it would be beyond foolish to let herself fall for a man who she already knew didn't plan to stay.

It didn't take Sullivan long to gather his belongings and check out of the Ponderosa Motel. He hadn't brought much when he'd first come to Bronco, because he hadn't planned to stay more than a few days. But those days had turned into weeks, and then weeks into months, forcing him to acquire a few more things. Still, as he retraced his earlier route to the Flying A, he wondered what it said about his life that he'd been able to put everything that mattered into a single suitcase and one cardboard box.

He found the cabin easily. It had more space than his apartment in Columbus, but somehow managed to feel cozier. There was a queen-sized bed in the bedroom— a definite upgrade from the double he'd been sleeping in at the motel—and a walk-in shower in the en suite bathroom. The kitchen was small but tidy. The appliances a little dated but clean. He realized he was going to have to get some groceries, which made him think of the trip he'd made to the store the day before—and making dinner with Sadie.

He'd wanted to share his good news with someone when Garrett offered him the job, and she was the first person who'd sprung to mind. Was it because she was the closest thing he had to a friend in Bronco? Or was there something more going on?

He wasn't looking for a romantic relationship, but there was something about Sadie that made him want to consider the possibility.

So after depositing his suitcase on the blanket chest at the foot of the bed, he got into his truck again and drove back to town.

It was almost five o'clock when he arrived at Sadie's Holiday House where she was gift-wrapping a purchase.

"I hope your sister likes the ornament," she said, as she affixed a bow to the top of the box.

"I know she will," the customer responded. "Because she picked it out when she was in here last weekend and sent me a photo with a text message that said, 'Christmas gift idea.' We've exchanged ornaments every Christmas for about ten years now, and Cassie has never been subtle about letting me know what she wants."

Sadie chuckled. "Well, Merry Christmas to both you and your sister."

"You'll be able to pass your wishes to her directly," the customer promised. "Because I picked out several ornaments that I like and sent photos to her."

"I'm happy to hear it."

"Merry Christmas," the customer said, and smiled at Sullivan as she walked past him on her way to the door.

Sadie smiled, too, as she came out from behind the counter. "People are going to start thinking you're a regular customer here—except that you always walk out of the shop empty-handed."

"Not always," he said.

Her smile faded a little as she remembered that he'd bought one of her wreaths for his brother's grave, and he was immediately sorry for dragging down the mood.

"How was your day today?" he asked, to steer the conversation in a different direction. "Did you have to deal with any crazy holiday shoppers?"

Her smile returned. "Thankfully, I don't get many of those. Instead, I get the shopper who's looking for something special or unique—not the hottest toy or latest tech. Although I am expecting a shipment of ugly sweaters tomorrow, and they're usually a hot ticket item."

"I don't doubt it," he said. "My mother has a whole drawer filled with those."

"Do they stay in the drawer or does she wear them?"

"She wears them. From December first through to the thirty-first."

"Then she'd undoubtedly appreciate it if you picked up another one for her," Sadie hinted.

"I don't know that I'm going to see her at Christmas this year."

She frowned. "You're not going to see your parents at Christmas?"

"I don't know," he said again.

"Well, whether you do or not, she'll want to celebrate when she does see you, and it would be nice if you had a gift for her. I'm expecting his and hers sizes, if you wanted one for your dad, too."

Coming from anyone else, it might have sounded like a sales pitch, but Sullivan knew that Sadie was more interested in him seeing his parents than pushing her merchandise.

"I can't imagine Lou Grainger in an ugly Christmas sweater," he said, sounding amused.

"How about an ugly Hanukkah sweater?"

He chuckled. "No."

"Does he have a sweet tooth?" she pressed. "Because we have these fabulous sugar cookies made by a local resident that are shaped and decorated like ugly Christmas sweaters."

"You're really pushing the ugly Christmas sweater theme," he noted.

"I like themes," she confided. "Last year, everyone on my gift list got something with a snowman on it."

"Well, maybe I'll stop by tomorrow to check out the sweaters," he decided.

"We're also getting ugly slippers, if that's more your dad's thing."

"If you'd ever met him, you'd know it's not."

Which was a strange thing to say, he realized. Obviously she'd never met his dad—she'd only met Sullivan ten days ago.

But even as the words spilled out of his mouth, he found himself wondering what she would think of his parents. He had no doubt that they would love Sadie.

She was sweet and warm and open—the type of woman anyone would love.

But it was unlikely that Lou and Ellie would ever have an opportunity to meet her. And even if they did, it wasn't as if he and Sadie were dating.

But they were becoming friends, and he was grateful for that.

"Maybe I should pick out some Christmas decorations," he said, shifting the conversation again.

"For your motel room?" she guessed.

"For my cabin."

A tiny pleat formed between her brows. "You moved into a cabin?"

"Onsite housing is one of the perks of working at the Flying A."

"You got the job?" she asked, her eyes going wide.

"I got the job," Sullivan confirmed, a smile spreading across his face.

"Congratulations." Sadie spontaneously threw her arms around him—and immediately realized the big hug was a big mistake.

Because suddenly their bodies were touching, her soft curves in contact with his hard muscles, causing heat to flood through her system, weakening her knees.

She hugged people all the time. Her mom. Her friends. Some of her regular customers even.

But this was different.

He was different.

Sure, she'd admitted to Evy that he was a good-looking man—and any woman could be forgiven for feeling a little tug of attraction when she was in the company of a good-looking man. But sitting across the table from Sullivan at DJ's or even working side-by-side with him in her kitchen couldn't in any way compare to the experience of pressing her body against his—as evidenced by the hormones suddenly rocketing through her system, urging her to move closer.

Instead, she drew back, feeling unaccustomedly self-conscious.

"Sorry." She offered him a fleeting smile. "I'm a hugger."

"Like Lotso?"

She couldn't hide her surprise at his question. "How do you know about Lotso?"

He shrugged. "A guy I used to work with has a seven-year-old daughter. Gracie was big on giving hugs to everyone she met, and when I asked her why, she told me she was like Lotso. Of course, I didn't have a clue what she was talking about, which is how I ended up sitting through the whole of *Toy Story 3* with her after a summer barbecue one Saturday night."

And didn't that story just melt her heart a little?

Because how could she resist a man who'd indulge a child in such a way?

But she had no business letting her heart melt. Especially not for this man. Not only because he had a lot of stuff to deal with, but also because he was Bobby's brother. And his new job at the Flying A was as temporary as his stay in Bronco.

Chapter Eight

"Let's go out and celebrate," Sullivan suggested.

"What did you have in mind?" Sadie asked.

"Pizza's always good for a celebration, and Bronco Brick Oven has the best in town."

And he really needed to get out of her shop before he gave in to the temptation to kiss her until they were both breathless.

Sadie had been nothing but kind to him since their first meeting, and he'd actually started to think that maybe they could be friends. But all it had taken was one quick hug and suddenly he was thinking *friends with benefits*, because the press of her soft curves against his body was the best thing he'd felt in a very long time.

Which was why he needed to take a step back, because hitting on Sadie didn't seem like an appropriate way to repay her friendship.

"That sounds great," she said. "Let me grab my phone so we can look at the menu and figure out what we want to order."

"Why can't we do that at the restaurant?" he wondered.

"Oh. I thought you were suggesting that we get takeout to eat at my place."

Her place? Where they'd be alone?

Nope.

Not a good idea.

"How is that going out to celebrate?" he asked lightly.

"I guess it's not," she admitted.

But there was something in her tone that made him ask, "Is there a reason you don't want to be seen in public with me?"

"Of course not," she immediately denied, though the flags of color that appeared high on her cheeks suggested otherwise.

"It was your idea that we have lunch together at DJ's," he remembered. "So why don't you want to go for pizza with me?"

"I didn't say that I didn't want to go," she hedged. "Only that I'd prefer takeout."

"Why?" he pressed.

"Because it's been a long day and I want to be able to take my boots off."

"You're a terrible liar, Sadie Chamberlin."

She huffed out a breath. "I hardly think that's a character flaw."

"It's certainly not," he agreed. "Now tell me the real reason that you don't want to go out."

This time her sigh was filled with resignation. "Because my mom's having dinner at Bronco Brick Oven tonight with some friends."

"And you think she'd object to you doing the same?"

"Of course not," she said again. "But I told you about her not-so-secret longing for grandchildren, and if she saw us together—her daughter having dinner with *a man*—she might misinterpret the nature of our relationship. And also…" she hesitated. "I'm a little worried about how she might react to seeing you, because you look so much like Bobby."

"Are you worried that she might faint?" he asked, only partly teasing.

"Well, she at least knows of your existence," Sadie said. "So probably not. But thinking of Bobby makes her think of Dana—not that she's ever *not* thinking of Dana—which makes her sad, and she was already a little out of sorts when she stopped by earlier today."

All of which made a strange kind of sense to him, and which meant abandoning his plan to take her out in public–where he wouldn't be tempted to kiss her or make any other inappropriate moves.

"Then I guess we better take a look at that takeout menu," he said, wishing he could order a side of self-restraint to go with their pizza.

"Are you sure you don't mind celebrating in?"

"I'm just happy to be celebrating with you," he said, and meant it.

So they ordered pizza and took it back to Sadie's house, where Elvis was waiting at the door.

Not completely alone, he noted, as the cat wound itself between his feet.

Unfortunately, the presence of a feline chaperone did nothing to banish the inappropriate thoughts that lingered in his mind after Sadie's hug.

"She's like an alarm clock," Sadie told Sullivan, as she poured the cat's kibble. "If her food isn't in her bowl at six thirty every day—a.m. *and* p.m.—she tracks me down to remind me that it's mealtime. And if I'm not home, she is *not* happy."

"How do you know she's not happy?" he asked curiously.

"She completely ignores me for the rest of the day—after she eats."

"Naturally," he agreed with a chuckle.

Having appeased the cat, Sadie washed her hands and retrieved plates from the cupboard. Then she grabbed a handful of napkins, one of which fluttered to the ground.

He started forward to pick it up, but Sadie had already bent over—an action that caused her skirt to stretch taut over her very shapely bottom. And though he knew he shouldn't be looking, he couldn't seem to tear his gaze away.

"What would you like to drink?" she asked, setting the plates and napkins on the table. "There are a couple of beers in the back of the fridge, if you want one. I've also got milk, juice and soda."

He cleared his throat. "Do you have Coke?"

"I do," she confirmed, pulling out two cans and setting them on the table.

While they ate, Sullivan recounted his interview with Garrett Abernathy and told Sadie how much he was looking forward to starting work after several months of unemployment.

She assured him that she could empathize. Although she admitted to enjoying her days off—especially those right after Christmas, when she was exhausted from the holiday rush—she couldn't imagine not having the store to keep her busy.

As they chatted, he found himself increasingly aware of Sadie's scrutiny. He wouldn't have minded so much if he'd thought she was checking him out, but he didn't think she was.

"You're looking at me like a scientist looks at a new discovery through a microscope," he finally remarked.

"Am I?" She gave him a quick, apologetic smile. "Sorry about that. I was just thinking that the physical resemblance between you and Bobby is startling, but the more time I spend with you, the more I realize that the similarities are only skin-deep."

"Why do you say that?" he asked, not just curious but also grateful for the change of topic, because talking about his brother wasn't likely to inspire lustful thoughts about Bobby's former sister-in-law.

"I don't know you very well, but you come across as a man who's strong and determined, while Bobby— though physically strong—always struck me as a little bit uncertain. More willing to follow the direction of another than forge his own path.

"And I'm hardly an expert in human behavior, so I'm really just guessing here," she continued, "but I suspect that's a reflection of your different upbringings."

"You're on the nurture side of the nature versus nurture debate?"

"No," she denied. Then reconsidered. "Or not always. But in this case, yes.

"And I know you're at odds with your mom and dad right now, but I get the impression, from what you've told me, that you grew up in a good home, with parents who always loved and supported you."

"And my brother wasn't so lucky?" he guessed, reaching into the box for another slice of pizza.

Sadie reached for the same slice at the same time. Their fingers brushed and sparks flew. She yanked her hand back, her eyes wide.

Yeah, there was definitely something between them—and she didn't look any happier to realize it than he'd been.

She took a slice from the opposite side of the pie and set it on her plate.

"Bobby didn't really have much of a family," she said, picking up the dropped thread of their conversation as if they hadn't just shared a tingling moment of awareness. As if she was totally unaffected by the accidental contact.

But the pulse point hammering in her throat told a different story.

"And he didn't like to talk about them, so most of what I know was told to me by my sister, and perhaps not entirely reliable," Sadie cautioned. "But according to Dana, he was primarily raised by his grandparents, though his mom lived with them, too, until he was about ten. That was when she took off for parts unknown and he never saw her again.

"It was something he and Dana had in common," she confided. "Each being abandoned by a parent."

"Was his dad in the picture?" he asked, following her lead in pretending the air around them wasn't suddenly crackling with electricity.

"I never heard any mention of his father. I'm not sure Bobby even knew who he was." She took a sip of her Coke. "Bobby's grandfather was a long-haul trucker and wasn't around that often, either. Probably a good thing, considering that he drank a lot when he was home—and the more he drank, the shorter his temper. But again, that's secondhand information."

"Do his grandparents still live in Bronco?"

Sadie shook her head. "His grandfather died when he was in high school, and his grandmother passed a few months after Bobby and Dana got married."

He sighed. "So there's no one left who could fill in the blanks about his family."

"I don't think so. Wait," she said, suddenly remembering. "There was an aunt. She came back for her mother's funeral, but she didn't stay long."

"I suppose it's too much to hope that you know the aunt's name and where she came back from?"

"I'm sorry," Sadie said. "Though you can probably do a search of birth records at town hall. Her parents were Delilah and Clayton Stone. Maybe look for their marriage certificate first, then birth records following that date."

"That's a good idea," he said.

And one he should have thought of himself before now. Since his arrival in Bronco, his emotions had been tangled up in knots, making it difficult for him to think about any of this rationally. And his sudden awareness of Sadie certainly wasn't helping to clear his mind.

But for now, he circled back to another comment she'd made.

"You said that you don't always believe nurture trumps nature," he noted. "Is that an insight into your own family?"

"My sister and I grew up in the same home, raised by the same single mom, yet we had very different personalities and values."

"You were ten when your dad walked out?"

"Dana was ten," she clarified. "I was seven."

"That must've been tough."

"It wasn't easy," she agreed. "Least of all for our mom, who worked multiple jobs to keep a roof over our heads and put food on the table.

"I tried to let her know how much I appreciated her efforts, helping out around the house so that she didn't have to cook and clean during those few hours that she was home every day, but my sister…"

"Wasn't so helpful?" he guessed.

"She was…unhappy with our situation. And never hesitated to express her feelings. Maybe she was angrier after our dad left. Maybe she took his rejection more personally. Maybe she really did think it was our mom's fault somehow." Sadie shrugged. "But instead of being grateful for everything that we had, she preferred to complain about what we didn't. Especially around Christmas, because her friends at school got all these big presents while we got a few essentials in our stockings, maybe some candy, and usually one or maybe two gifts under the tree.

"It never really bothered me that our Christmases were modest, because it was still Christmas—a day to celebrate as a family. And one of the rare occasions that our mom was home with us all day."

"You celebrated to the fullest," he noted. "And now, through Sadie's Holiday House, you help others do the same."

"I guess I do." She smiled, as if pleased by his remark.

And he was pleased that he'd been able to make her smile.

"Speaking of work—we both have jobs to go to tomorrow," he pointed out reluctantly.

"We do," she agreed. "And I bet your day is going to start earlier than mine."

"Six a.m." He pushed away from the table. "Actually, I'm supposed to be working by six, so I'll have to be up by five if I want breakfast and my caffeine fix before then.

"Another reason to be grateful that lodging was included with the job, so that I don't have to drive fifteen miles out to the ranch at the beginning and end of each day."

"I like being able to walk to work," Sadie said. "Especially after a snowstorm—and we have our fair share of those in Bronco—because I only have to worry about shoveling my steps before heading out for the day. And by the time I get home, my neighbor has usually cleared my driveway with his snowblower."

He stacked their plates and carried them to the sink. "We should all have such neighbors."

"Believe me, I know how lucky I am." She dumped their empty cans into the recycle bin under the sink. "Thank you for dinner—*again*."

"My pleasure."

"Wait," she said, as he started toward the door.

He paused, equal parts hopeful and fearful that she might want to hug him again.

"Aren't you going to take the leftover pizza?" she asked.

He shook his head. "You can keep it."

"I've still got leftover stir-fry in my fridge."

"Fine, I'll take the pizza," he agreed. "But only because I don't have any groceries at the cabin, so it'll be my first breakfast in my new place."

"You can't have pizza for breakfast," she protested, starting to pull the box away from him. "Let me give you some bread or cereal or—"

"Pizza is fine," he assured her. "After work tomorrow, I'll hit the grocery store for the essentials."

"Don't forget to stop by my shop, too," she said, finally relinquishing her hold on the box. "To check out the ugly Christmas sweaters."

"I won't forget," he promised.

"Then I'll see you tomorrow."

"You'll see me tomorrow," he confirmed.

She smiled then, and *damn* if that smile didn't fill his chest with an unexpected warmth.

He drove away from Sadie's house, already counting the hours until he would see her again.

Tuesday afternoon, Sullivan stopped by Holiday House, as promised, and picked out an ugly Christmas sweater for his mom. He seemed happy with his choice—and even happier to learn that the shop offered complimentary gift-wrapping. But as Sadie was on her own with several other customers in the store, he opted to pick it up another day. She didn't protest because that meant she could look forward to seeing him again later in the week.

Wednesday, she took Elvis and a tray of lasagna to her mom's apartment for their scheduled tree decorating. The cat wasn't particularly fond of car rides, but she was fond of Roberta, and Sadie figured that would balance things out. Plus, she felt guilty that she'd been neglecting her feline companion as a result of long hours at the shop—and spending time with Sullivan.

While stringing garland and hanging ornaments, she had a nice visit with her mom, and Sadie was happy to note that Roberta was in better spirits when her tree was up and the lights were twinkling.

Thursday was chaos from beginning to end, starting with a text message from Lynda to let her know that she couldn't work that day because her daughter was home from school with a fever. Sadie could have called Beth to fill in, but she knew that her other regular employee was busy with card orders, so she tried Noah and Tanya, the high school students she'd hired as seasonal help. Unfortunately, they were both unavailable, leaving Sadie on her own.

Which, if she'd only had to deal with customers, wouldn't have been a big deal. But of course it was the day that she also received the wrong shipment from one of her suppliers, so she had to make arrangements to send it back and ensure her original order would be filled. Then one of her patrons let her four-year-old daughter use the bathroom while she stood outside chatting with a neighbor, and the little girl used so much paper she clogged the toilet.

It wasn't the first time she'd had to deal with plumbing issues, so she knew a good plumber—Evy's father, Owen Roberts. Thankfully, he had the toilet working again in short order, but by the end of the day, Sadie was completely tapped out. Finally, when the clock turned to 6:00 p.m., she turned the Open sign to Closed and locked the door.

Things were mostly back to normal on Friday. Lynda showed up on time for her usual shift (although her daughter was still sick, Lynda's mother-in-law was babysitting), but by lunchtime, everyone was buzzing about the big storm that was supposed to blow through and speculating that schools might be closed early. Sure enough, Lynda got a call around two o'clock and left to pick up her son.

Apparently, most of the residents of Bronco had heeded the storm warnings, because there was an almost two-hour stretch after Lynda had gone that no customers ventured into the store. Not until Gloria Bell walked through the door.

"Looks like the weather forecast was right," Gloria remarked, as she carried her basket to the checkout counter. "The snow is really starting to come down out there."

"It would look awfully strange if it was going up, wouldn't it?" Sadie responded cheekily.

Her customer chuckled, then wagged an admonishing finger. "Don't you go underestimating Mother Nature."

"I wouldn't dare," she promised, as she scanned the woman's purchases.

"You should think about closing up early." Gloria offered her credit card as payment. "You're not going to get any customers in this weather."

"And yet, here you are."

"Because you're on my way home from work, which is where I'm going as soon as I leave here."

Sadie finished bagging Gloria's items and slid the bag across the counter. "You drive safely now. And Merry Christmas."

"I'll say Merry Christmas to you, too," Gloria said. "But you know I'm going to be back at least one more time before the holiday."

Sadie smiled. "I sure hope so."

She walked her customer out, pausing at the door for a moment to watch the snow swirling outside.

It probably wouldn't hurt to close the shop early, she acknowledged. The streets were mostly deserted and those who were out and about seemed to be hurrying toward their homes—pedestrians slipping and sliding on the snow-covered walks and cars skidding on the icy roads. Even Bean & Biscotti had closed early, making Sadie suspect that hers was the last shop standing on the strip.

But she kept the Open sign in the window for now, because she planned to stick around for a while, anyway, tidying up displays that had been rearranged by customers, restocking depleted shelves and packaging orders that needed to be shipped.

The snow was coming down even more heavily now, but snow in December was hardly anything new. The winds, however, were significantly fiercer than usual, howling in the darkness and making the windows rattle. Sadie rubbed her hands briskly up and down her arms as she moved across the room to nudge the thermostat up a little.

At six o'clock, she locked the door. Gloria had been right—no one else had wandered into the store after she'd gone. And Sadie was glad, because the storm had intensified to the point that visibility was practically nonexistent.

She'd walked the route to and from her shop so many times she'd often said she could do so with her eyes closed. But blinded by snow and pushed off course by the wind was another matter, and she wasn't foolish enough to attempt even that short trek in the current weather.

She would sleep on the floor if she had to and, until then, she had more than enough to keep her busy.

At least until the power went out.

Chapter Nine

Dammit. The phone lines were down.

Sullivan had tried to call Sadie's Holiday House, to see if she was still there, but he kept getting an automated message that the number was not in service.

The next logical step would be to call her cell phone—but he didn't have her number. Because in all the time that they'd spent together, they'd never exchanged numbers.

He didn't realize that he was scowling at his phone until Crosby Abernathy asked, "Something wrong?"

After a full day's work, he and Garrett's next-to-youngest brother were the only two ranch hands left in the barn, having just returned from fixing a section of downed fence after everyone else had already taken shelter from the storm in their respective homes.

Sullivan tucked the phone into his back pocket. "I was trying to reach a friend in town, but the phone lines seem to be down."

"That happens when we get storms like this."

"Yeah."

"You're worried about this friend?" Crosby guessed.

"Yeah," he said again.

"Hopefully not worried enough to think about venturing out in this mess."

"I'm not just thinking about it, I'm going to do it," Sullivan decided. "I won't be able to sleep tonight if I don't know that she's okay."

Not that he had any reason to think that Sadie wasn't okay, but he knew that he wouldn't be able to think about anything else until he knew for sure that she was safe.

"She must be someone special to have you all tied up in knots like this," Crosby mused.

"She doesn't... I'm not..." He huffed out a breath. "I'm just worried about her."

"Sure." The other man nodded his understanding.

"I should be back in a few hours. For sure before six tomorrow morning."

"Stay safe," Crosby said. "If the roads are bad—and they probably will be—don't worry about rushing back here."

"Thanks, boss." Sullivan's response caught on the wind, because he was already halfway out the door.

It wasn't only Boy Scouts who knew how to be prepared, Sadie mused, as she turned on the battery-operated lantern she'd retrieved from a cabinet in the kitchen.

Roberta had taught both her daughters more than cooking and cleaning. She'd showed them how to hang a curtain rod, caulk around a window and even fix a leaky faucet. She'd ensured that they knew how to change a flat tire, use a fire extinguisher and perform basic first aid. She certainly wasn't a woman who would cower in the darkness—and neither was Sadie.

But knowing how competent and capable her mom was didn't prevent Sadie from worrying about her. Especially as it was Friday, and Roberta always worked the dinner shift at the diner on Fridays. Not that Sadie imagined many residents had ventured out to eat on a night like tonight—not even for the diner's legendary meatloaf and mashed potatoes—and she had to trust that Wayne would have sent his employees home early when the weather started to turn.

Still, she'd feel better if she actually talked to her mom and knew that she was safe, so she was relieved when Roberta answered her cell phone on the second ring.

"Are you home?" she asked.

"I'm home," her mom confirmed. "Wayne watched the snow pile up for more than an hour before he realized that he'd better let everyone go home or he'd be trapped at the diner with us."

"I'm glad you're safe."

"Are you?" Roberta asked.

"I'm safe," she said. "But I'm still at the shop, and I'm going to stay right here until the storm has passed."

"You might be there all night," her mom warned.

"I don't mind. The shop only has ghosts in the fall during the run up to Halloween."

"But do you have power?" Roberta asked, not amused by Sadie's attempted humor.

"No," she said again. "That went out just before I called you."

"Which means your furnace is out, too."

"Yeah, but I've got a whole shelf filled with ugly Christmas sweaters that I can layer on if I start to feel cold."

"And blankets, too," Roberta remembered. "I saw a lovely display of them when I was there on Monday."

"That's true," Sadie confirmed. "So there's no reason for you to worry about me."

"I'm a mom. Worrying is what I do best."

"Well, my cell phone is almost fully charged, so you should be able to reach me if you need to. But I'm going to say goodbye for now to preserve as much battery as possible."

"Okay," Roberta said. "Stay safe and remember I love you."

"You, too, Mom." She disconnected and tucked her phone in her pocket.

Maybe it was because there was so much of her heart and soul in the shop, but it never bothered Sadie to be there alone—even in the dark. And why would it when she knew every nook and cranny, every creaking floorboard and dark corner? Holiday House wasn't just her business, it was her happy place, where she was enveloped by the familiar scents of spiced apple cider and fresh gingerbread and surrounded by elements of the happiest time of the year—all year round.

In fact, she was perfectly content to putter around the shop in the quiet—until someone started banging on the door.

Then her heart started pounding frantically against her ribs, as if trying to break out of her chest.

Because it was one thing to be alone in the shop and quite another to have her solitude interrupted by a potential stranger seeking shelter from the storm.

She knew it would be foolish to open the door.

On the other hand, would she be able to forgive herself if she ignored the summons and it turned out that whoever was on the other side ended up perishing in the storm?

With a weary sigh—and more than a little bit of trepidation—she ventured cautiously toward the front of the shop, leaving the lantern on the counter so as not to illuminate her approach.

"Sadie! Sadie! Are you in there?"

Recognition—and relief—made her knees weak.

It wasn't an unknown someone at the door.

It was Sullivan.

"Sadie, if you're in there, open the damn door!"

She pulled the key out of her pocket and unlocked the damn door, pushing it open to allow him entry—and shelter from the raging storm.

"What are you doing here?" she asked, as he stomped the snow off his boots.

He peered at her from beneath the snow-covered

brim of his Stetson. "What am I *doing* here?" His tone was incredulous. "I came to see if you were okay."

"Why wouldn't I be okay?"

"Because it seems like half the town is without power and you're alone here in the dark."

"It's not completely dark." She gestured toward the lantern that bathed the checkout counter in a pool of light. "I have a lantern."

"You have a lantern."

"And spare batteries," she added.

"And spare batteries," he echoed.

"I know how to take care of myself, and I'm fine," she assured him.

"You're fine."

She frowned. "Why are you repeating everything I'm saying?"

"Because I was worried about you!"

She knew that she should appreciate his concern, but she certainly didn't appreciate being shouted at.

"And you're disappointed that I'm not huddled in a corner, shivering with fear because the lights are out?" she challenged.

"Of course not!" he snapped.

"Then why are you yelling at me?"

"I don't know!"

She folded her arms over her chest.

He huffed out a breath. "Okay, maybe I thought you'd be pleased to see me."

"I'm always happy to see you. But I don't like the idea of you—or anyone—venturing out in this weather to check on me."

"Maybe I did want to rescue you," he reluctantly acknowledged.

"And I ruined your white knight routine by not playing the role of the damsel in distress," she realized.

The furrow between his brows deepened. "I'd never pretend to be a white knight."

"And yet you came here to rescue me."

"Because…"

She waited for him to finish his explanation.

Instead, Sullivan cursed under his breath, then hauled her into his arms and crushed his mouth down on hers.

Sadie should have known that he'd be as confident when making a move on a woman as he was in everything else he did.

Not that she'd ever imagined him kissing her.

She might have dreamed about it, but only because she couldn't control her dreams. When she was awake, however, she didn't let her heart yearn for things she was sure she could never have. She'd been certain that Sullivan was one of those things—a man unreachable and unattainable.

But her heart did yearn for him.

It was a simple fact she couldn't deny now that his arms were around her, holding her close, and his mouth was moving over hers.

He was a man who knew how to kiss a woman, she noted with pleasure. A man who could take a woman to the edge of seduction with nothing more than the skillful pressure of his mouth. And right now, he was nibbling and licking and savoring, as if he had all the time in the world and wanted to spend every minute of it kissing her.

Sadie lifted her arms to link them behind his head, her fingers sifting through the silky hair at the back of his neck as she kissed him back with equal focus and attention. She'd been kissed by other men, touched by other men, loved by other men. But no other man had made her feel a fraction of the want that pulsed in her veins and the need that clawed at her belly.

The intensity of her desire for Sullivan wasn't only unprecedented, it was a little bit scary. Because she knew that if she let herself fall for him, he would break her heart. Because he wasn't going to stay in Bronco, and she couldn't imagine a life anywhere else.

But he was here now, and she couldn't bring herself to pull away. To let him go. To relinquish this exquisite pleasure, a respite from the storm, a stolen moment in the dark.

But then it wasn't dark any longer.

Though her eyes were closed, she immediately knew that the lights had come back on. Or maybe it was the sound of the furnace kicking in that revealed the power had been restored.

Sullivan must have heard it, too, because he drew back then, easing his lips from hers and exhaling a shuddery sigh.

For a moment, the only sounds in the room were the hum of the furnace and their labored breathing.

"I was worried about you," he finally said.

"You said that already."

They fell quiet again.

"You could have called," she pointed out, breaking the silence.

"I tried," he told her. "The phone lines are down."

"I still have cell service."

"I don't have your cell phone number."

"Oh. I guess we should probably exchange numbers."

He opened his phone, added her name to his contacts, then offered it to her to input her number. She did so, then sent a text message to herself from his phone so that she would have his. Then she picked up her phone and replied to the message.

Sullivan took his phone back, his lips curving as he read the brief exchange.

R U OK?

I'm ok. No need to worry.

"FYI, I would never ask are you okay in only four letters."

"And yet, you just said FYI."

"So I did," he acknowledged. "Also FYI, that kiss totally made my trip into town worthwhile."

Pleasure filled her heart, even as her brain urged caution. "But now you have to drive all the way back to the ranch in this mess."

"Eventually."

"Anyway," she said, "the power's back on and you've seen for yourself that I'm okay, so there's no reason for you to worry."

"The snow's still coming down pretty hard out there."

"I don't plan on going anywhere right now," she assured him.

"Then I guess I'm not going anywhere, either," he decided.

"You want to hang out here with me?"

"Actually, yeah, I do," he said, sounding a little surprised by the admission.

"In that case, do you want a cup of coffee?" she asked.

"Coffee sounds good," he said.

She led him to the kitchen at the rear of the shop.

He took off his snow-dusted jacket and hung it on the back of one of the chairs to dry.

Since her body was feeling very warm after the hot kiss they'd shared, Sadie peeled off the Christmas sweater she was wearing—and then another one that was beneath it to reveal a third sweater.

Glancing up, she saw that his eyes were on her, his gaze hot. "I'm waiting to see how many more layers you're going to remove," he said.

She swallowed. "That's all." Her voice shook a little when she wanted to sound firm. Because she knew it wouldn't take many more kisses for him to convince her to discard every last stitch she was wearing. "This sweater is mine. Those I borrowed from inventory to keep me warm when the power was out.

"And before you ask, you don't need to worry that one of them might have been your mom's. Hers was already boxed and wrapped, safe from my scavenger hunt."

"I wasn't worried," he assured her.

She filled the reservoir with water and put a filter

in the basket, then reached into the cupboard for the coffee.

"Regular or decaf?" she asked.

He shrugged. "Either works for me."

"Let's go with half caff," she said, putting a scoop of each into the filter.

A few minutes later, they were sitting at the table with their coffee and cookies when the phone rang.

"Apparently, the landlines have been restored," Sullivan commented, as she rose from the table to answer the call.

"Hello?"

"I was just checking to see if you were still at the shop," Roberta said.

Sadie wasn't surprised to hear her mom's voice on the other end of the line. She couldn't imagine anyone else calling at such a late hour.

"I told you I wasn't going anywhere," Sadie reminded her.

"You're holding up okay?"

"I'm fine, Mom. How are *you*?"

"I'm good," Roberta said. "In fact, we're just about to play another round of canasta."

"Who's *we*?"

"Me and Ingrid Lindgren and Hazel Fast and Ron Dulik. They all came over here when the power went out."

"I hope you weren't playing cards in the dark."

"We weren't," Roberta said. "We had candles."

Sadie slapped her palm against her forehead. "Is your power back on now?"

"It is," her mom confirmed. "And the Christmas lights are on, and everyone agrees that the tree looks beautiful."

"I'm glad."

"Hazel's son drives a snowplow. She can send him over to pick you up, if you want to go home."

"Thanks, but I'm sure his time would be better spent actually plowing the streets."

"He's a nice young man," Roberta said, then dropped her voice a little to add, "And single."

"He's divorced. *Twice*. With two kids with each of his ex-wives."

"I know. Hazel was just showing me the latest pictures of her grandkids."

"I'm going to hang up now, Mom."

"Don't be so quick to—"

"I love you, Mom. Goodbye."

She replaced the receiver and turned back to the table to find Sullivan watching her, a smirk on his face.

Chapter Ten

"My mom worries about me," Sadie felt compelled to explain.

"Apparently she also wants to set you up with a twice-divorced snowplow operator with four kids," Sullivan remarked, sounding amused.

She felt her cheeks burn. "Obviously you could hear both sides of the conversation."

"It was entertaining."

"I'm sure it was." She returned to her seat at the table and picked up her mug.

"Does she live close to you?" he asked, reaching into the tin for a cookie.

"Not too far." Sadie smiled wryly. "And sometimes not nearly far enough."

He chuckled at that.

"I actually bought the house on Meadowlark Street for us to live in together, but she refused to move out of her apartment."

"I didn't realize you owned your house," he said. "I assumed it was a rental."

She shook her head. "It was always one of my life goals to own my own house. We lost ours when my dad left," she confided. "The mortgage and upkeep were more than my mom could handle, even working three jobs. When the bank threatened to foreclose on the mortgage, she decided to sell the house so that we'd at least get *something* out of it. She put that something aside for Dana and me, for college, and we moved into a two-bedroom basement apartment.

"I hated that apartment. It was dark and gloomy— and I had to share a room with Dana, who hated even more that she had to share a room with me. Thankfully, we were only there for about six months before my mom found a place in a newer building, closer to our school and an easy commute to her jobs.

"It was still a two-bedroom, but she gave us the bigger bedroom. Two years after that, we moved into a three-bedroom apartment in the same building. When Dana and Bobby got married, we downsized to a two-bedroom again.

"My mom still lives in that same apartment, apparently very happily," she acknowledged ruefully. "She insists that she's comfortable and content there and that I need to live my own life without my mother underfoot all the time."

She chose a cookie and nibbled on the edge.

"At the time, I wasn't just disappointed, I was actually kind of annoyed," she confessed.

"You were annoyed that your mom was giving you space to live your own life?"

"I didn't see it that way back then. I saw it as me wanting to take care of her, the way she'd always taken care of Dana and me, and her rejecting my efforts."

"And now?" he prompted.

"Now, I appreciate that owning a house can be a lot of work. Especially when it comes to repairs and outdoor maintenance. But even so, I really do love having a place of my own."

"I have a condo in Columbus for exactly the reasons you mentioned," he told her. "Working as an engineer, I didn't have the time for maintenance and repairs—or maybe I just didn't want to be bothered. But I didn't figure on living there forever. Only until I met someone special, fell in love, got married, and had a couple of kids." He sipped his coffee, shrugged. "Except that, so far, none of that's happened."

"You've never been married?" she asked.

He shook his head. "I've had a few long-term relationships, but they inevitably fizzled when I hesitated to take the next step. I'm not afraid to make a commitment. I'm just not willing to make one until I know for sure that I've met the woman I want to be with for the rest of my life."

She popped the last bit of cookie into her mouth, surprised by his revelation. "Are you saying that you believe everyone has a perfect match out there somewhere?"

"I don't know that anyone has a *perfect* match,"

he said. "But I believe that when you meet the right person—or at least someone you can tolerate for the duration—you'll know it."

"Tolerate?" Sadie echoed, shaking her head.

He grinned. "'Till death do us part' can be a long time, so you better hope you can tolerate the one you're exchanging vows with."

"I would hope you'd love the one you're exchanging vows with," she said dryly.

"Well, that, too," he agreed. "But love has ups and downs, while tolerance can help a relationship endure."

"You're going to sweep some lucky woman off her feet with romantic words like that," she said dryly.

"You don't think, 'I can tolerate you and want to marry you' are the words to win a woman's heart?" he asked, tongue-in-cheek.

"Only a very desperate woman," she assured him.

He chuckled. "The truth is, I have pretty high standards when it comes to relationships, because of my parents."

"They're getting ready to celebrate fifty years of marriage, so obviously they've done something right."

"They've done a lot of things right," he confirmed. "I'm not saying they never argue, because of course they do, but each one always supports the other and they are undoubtedly committed to one another, and I've never been willing to settle for anything less than that."

"And you shouldn't," Sadie agreed, pleased to hear—in his words and his tone—the obvious love and affection he had for his parents despite their current estrangement.

"What about you?" Sullivan asked. "Do you have everything you ever wanted?"

"With respect to my career, absolutely," she said. "My personal life is another matter. I haven't completely given up hope, but there aren't a lot of marriage-minded single guys of an appropriate age in Bronco."

"Maybe you should look outside of Bronco," he suggested.

"I've thought about it, but my home and my business are here," she reminded him. "And I'm leery of long-distance relationships. Or maybe I'm just leery of relationships in general."

"Why's that?"

"Because if there's one thing I've learned, it's that men don't stick around."

"You're talking about your dad," he guessed.

"He was only the first one who walked away," she told him.

"How many more have there been?"

"Two," she said. "Which maybe doesn't seem like a lot, but there's a definite pattern."

"Tell me about them," he suggested.

"You really want to know?"

"I wouldn't have asked if I didn't."

"Okay, Michael DeMille was the first boy I loved. We were together all through our junior and senior years of high school, then he left Bronco to go to MIT and never came back."

"That probably happens more often than not—high school sweethearts going their separate ways after graduation."

"I know," she admitted. "But we didn't go our separate ways—he left and I stayed.

"Several years after Michael had gone, I met Harlow Windsor. After dating for a year and a half, we moved in together and he starting dropping hints that a proposal was coming. Six weeks after that, he was offered a promotion that required him to move to California."

"You didn't want to go with him?"

"And leave all this?" She gestured around her, then shook her head. "No, I didn't want to go with him. But the truth is, he never even asked. He just told me he was leaving, and that was that. One day, we were talking about getting married and the next day, he was gone."

Sullivan shook his head and muttered an uncomplimentary name for her ex under his breath before asking, "Were you heartbroken?"

She hesitated for half a second before responding with a sigh. "No," she said again. "Which only proves that any dreams I had about marrying him and having a family with him were doomed to fail, because obviously I didn't really love him."

Still, it had hurt when he'd left.

Just as she knew it would hurt again when Sullivan left, if she was foolish enough to let herself love him.

With that realization weighing heavily on her heart, she finished her coffee then stood up and made her way to the back door, cupping her hands against the glass to peer out into the night. "The snow doesn't look like it's going to let up anytime soon and the roads are completely impassable now," she said when she turned back to face him.

"Then I guess we're going to be here a while." He carried both of their mugs to the sink and rinsed them under the tap.

"I feel bad that you're stuck."

He dried his hands on a towel. "If I could choose to be alone in my cabin or here with you, I'd definitely choose here with you," he told her.

"Really?"

"Really," he said, and lowered his head to kiss her again.

But this time his mouth feathered over the curve of her cheek, then the line of her jaw and the point of her chin. It was a caress more than a kiss, incredibly sensual and unbelievably arousing. Finally his lips found and covered her own, and his tongue swept over the seam of her lips. She answered the wordless question with a sigh that parted her lips, welcomed the deepening of the kiss. As their tongues danced together, his hands moved over her, sliding up her back, down her arms, making her shiver.

"You're cold." He whispered the words against her lips.

"No." She pressed closer to him. "I'm not cold."

How could she be cold when there was so much heat coursing through her veins? So much heat, she was surprised that her bones didn't melt, leaving her in a puddle on the floor.

After several more minutes—hours? days?—he groaned and tore his mouth from hers. "I'm sorry."

She swallowed. "Why are you sorry?"

He rubbed the curve of her bottom lip with the pad of his thumb. "For coming on too strong. Moving too fast."

"You didn't. You're not." She blew out a breath. "But maybe, considering the time and place, we should take a step back."

"That's probably a good idea."

"And try to get some sleep."

"Another good idea." He looked around the tiny kitchen. "But where?"

She led him back to the front room and stopped by a stack of Christmas throws. She spread one out on the floor, tossed a couple of decorative pillows at one end, then shook out another blanket as a cover.

"I feel like a six-year-old at a sleepover," Sullivan said, stretching out on top of the blanket. "Except that I never wanted to cuddle with any of my friends back then."

"Cuddling helps preserve body heat," Sadie said, wiggling closer to him until her back was aligned with his front.

"At the expense of my sanity," he muttered, covering them with the second throw.

"Do you want me to take my blanket and pillow to the other side of the room?"

In answer to her question, he wrapped an arm around her, holding her in place. "Sanity's overrated."

Sadie fell asleep in his arms, with a smile on her face and happiness in her heart.

From somewhere in the distance, Sullivan registered familiar beeping and scraping sounds. Snowplows, he realized. A telltale sign that the worst of the storm had passed and crews were out clearing the roads.

He shifted and groaned, his body protesting the use of the floor as a bed. Then Sadie rolled over to snuggle against him, and his aching muscles forgot all about the hard floor in favor of her soft body.

Her eyes opened slowly and blinked in the darkness. "Is it morning?"

"Very early morning."

She pushed away the blanket and eased herself into a sitting position. "When I first took over the shop, two of the rooms upstairs were still furnished as bedrooms. I got rid of the furniture to make room for more inventory. A decision I never regretted…until last night."

He chuckled as he rose to his feet and offered her a hand. "Well, you'll be able to sleep in your own bed tonight."

"But first, I have to get through the day." She shook out one of the blankets they'd used and began to fold it.

"I'd suggest that you keep the shop closed today, but then you'd remind me how many days there are until Christmas—"

"Fifteen," she interjected. "Which is why keeping the shop closed is not an option."

"How about opening late?" He picked up the pillows, embroidered with the words *Merry Christmas* on one side and *Bah, Humbug* on the other, and tossed them into the bin filled with other pillows.

"That might be unavoidable." She stacked the second blanket on top of the first. "Because I definitely have to shower and change before I interact with any customers."

"And I need to be heading to the ranch," he said. "But I'll give you a ride home first."

"I'm happy to walk."

"But I wouldn't be happy knowing you were trudging through the two-and-a-half feet of snow on the sidewalks," he told her.

"I have a spare pair of boots in the back," she told him.

"Two-and-a-half feet of snow," he repeated.

"Okay," she relented. "If you're not in too much of a hurry, you can give me a ride home."

"I'm not in too much of a hurry."

So she retrieved her coat and her purse and had her keys in hand when he drew her into his arms.

"What are you doing?" she asked warily.

"I want to kiss you goodbye."

"You just said you were going to drive me home," she reminded him.

"I am. But I didn't know if you'd let me kiss you in front of your house where any of your neighbors might see."

"I doubt any of them will be out and about this early," she said. "But I'm also not going to let you kiss me before I've had a chance to brush my teeth or—"

He decided the quickest—and most satisfying—way to silence her was with his lips.

He wasn't surprised that she balked at first, pressing her lips firmly together. But he knew how to be patient when patience was required, and eventually she yielded and kissed him back.

"If we don't go now, we're both going to be late," she cautioned several minutes later.

So he went out to brush the snow off his truck while Sadie locked up the shop. Less than five minutes later, he was pulling up in front of her house.

"Thanks for the ride," she said. "And the company last night."

"It was my pleasure."

"You enjoyed sleeping on the floor?"

"Let's say the pleasure was greater than the pain," he amended.

She smiled. "I thought so, too."

"Wait," he said as she reached for the door handle.

Sadie paused.

"I was thinking about dinner."

"Really? I was thinking about breakfast."

He chuckled. "I meant tonight. I'd like to take you out."

Her heart gave a happy little skip, but she managed to keep her voice level when she asked, "Are you asking me on a date?"

"I am."

Another little skip, and this time, she couldn't hold back the smile that curved her lips. Because Sullivan was asking her on a date—and, at the moment, she couldn't imagine anything that would make her happier.

"The shop doesn't close until six," she reminded him.

"Should I pick you up there at six thirty?"

"You can pick me up here at six thirty."

"Because you have to feed Elvis," he suddenly remembered.

She nodded.

He brushed another quick kiss over her lips. "See you then."

Chapter Eleven

Sadie practically floated through the rest of the day.

Well, first she shoveled her porch and front steps, then she showered and changed and hurried back to the shop, and *then* she floated through the rest of the day.

It was a slow morning at Holiday House as most of the town was still digging itself out from the snow, but around midday, business started to pick up. And everyone who came in was talking about the storm—where they were when it hit; whether they lost power and for how long; how deep were the snowdrifts in their yards.

"Poor Chester couldn't even get down the back steps to pee," Janice Ferris lamented.

"And to think you paid to have him neutered in the fall," Amy Marconi replied. "When the snow could have just frozen his balls off."

Sadie had to turn away so the two women didn't see that she was trying not to laugh at their conversation.

Around three o'clock, Evy came in and, noting that Beth was working the register and Tanya was circulating on the floor, grabbed her friend by the arm and dragged her to the kitchen.

"What's up?" Sadie asked.

"That's what I want to know," Evy told her. "When I was in Bean & Biscotti this morning, I heard Lucy Connor tell Miranda Johnston that her husband saw Sullivan Grainger's truck parked outside your store at three o'clock this morning."

"What was Lucy Connor's husband doing out at three o'clock in the morning in the middle of a blizzard?"

"That's a good question," her friend acknowledged. "But not the one I'm interested in knowing the answer to right now."

"So what's your question?" Sadie asked.

"Were you stuck here last night? And was Sullivan with you?"

"I wouldn't say I was stuck so much as I chose not to venture out into the storm to go home," she hedged. "And Sullivan came by to check on me, because he couldn't get through when the phone lines were down, then decided to wait out the storm with me."

"So the two of you were here together?" Evy said, pressing for clarification. "All night?"

"We were," Sadie confirmed.

"Did you…?" Her friend waggled her eyebrows.

"No!" Not that Sadie hadn't given the possibility some very serious thought, though admitting as much to Evy would only lead to more questions. "But…he kissed me."

A smile spread across her friend's face. "And?" she prompted. "Did his kiss make your toes curl?"

"My toes couldn't curl," she confided, "because everything inside me completely melted."

"Oh, wow." Evy fanned her face with a hand. "So… why didn't you…?"

"Aside from the fact that I've known the man all of two weeks, this shop isn't exactly set up for seduction."

"Where there's a will, there's a way." Evy flattened her palms on the bistro table, testing its strength, and frowned when it wobbled. "And there's plenty of floor space."

"Which we used to sleep on," Sadie told her friend.

"So if you didn't…"

"We didn't," she said again. Firmly.

"Then what *did* you do all night?"

"We talked for a long time, then fell asleep. This morning, he drove me home and went back to the Flying A."

"Did he kiss you again before he left?"

"He kissed me again," she confided. "And…he's taking me out for dinner tonight."

"Where's he taking you?"

"I didn't think to ask," Sadie admitted.

"Because it doesn't matter, right? Because all that matters is that you're going to see him again. *Because you're in love*," her friend concluded in a singsong voice.

Sadie rolled her eyes in response to Evy's teasing. "I'm *not* in love."

But she knew that she could easily let herself fall for Sullivan. And she was desperately trying to hold herself back—because no matter how much of a connection she and Sullivan seemed to have, he didn't plan to stay in Bronco.

When he got the answers he wanted about Bobby and Bobby's death, he'd go back to Columbus. Back to his job, his condo, his family.

He would leave her, just as her father and Michael and Harlow had all left her.

And accepting that inevitability, it would be beyond foolish to let herself fall in love with him, perpetuating the cycle of abandonment she desperately wanted to break so that she might find her own happily-ever-after.

Which made her wonder—what was she doing with Sullivan?

Why had she accepted his invitation to dinner tonight?

Why was she opening herself up to the possibility— no, the certainty—of heartache again?

Those were the questions that plagued her throughout the rest of the afternoon and even after she'd gone home to get ready for her date.

Unfortunately, the answers were simple and undeniable. Because she couldn't bring herself to pull away from him. Because she really liked him. Because she really wanted him to be *the one*.

Or maybe it had just been a really long time since

she'd been with a man, and Sullivan's kisses tempted her more than she wanted to admit.

I'm not afraid to make a commitment, he'd told her. *I'm just not willing to make one until I know for sure that I've met the woman I want to be with for the rest of my life.*

Why couldn't she be that woman? Sadie wondered.

If his kisses were any indication, he was obviously attracted to her. And he seemed to enjoy spending time with her. He'd even gone out of his way—potentially risking his life—to check on her in the storm.

Or maybe she was simply convenient to him right now. Someone he could spend time with rather than be alone. Maybe she didn't mean anything more to him than that.

She tossed that depressing thought aside along with the Christmas sweater she'd worn to work then shimmied out of the long chambray skirt, exchanging them for a soft blue V-neck sweater that was much more flattering and the pretty skirt Evy had given her.

Though the outfit wasn't so very different from what she wore every day, it felt good to change, brush out her hair, dab on some lip gloss and spritz on her favorite perfume. Then she added a pair of low-heeled boots and replaced her tacky (but adorable) Christmas-light earrings with the simple gold hoops that had been a high school graduation present from her mom.

Sullivan knocked on the door promptly at six thirty, just as she was feeding Elvis.

"You're punctual," she said. "I like that in a man."

"You're beautiful," he said. "I like that in a woman."

The words might have been easy to dismiss, if not for the obvious appreciation in his eyes as they moved over her.

"You clean up nicely, too, cowboy."

"I am a cowboy, aren't I?" he said, grinning. "Well, at least for the time being."

The casual reminder that his position at the Flying A—and even his presence in Bronco—was only temporary might have caused her mood to dip again, except that he leaned forward and brushed his lips against hers.

It wasn't a deep or passionate kiss but one that spoke of easy affection, and it filled her heart with joy.

"Are you hungry?" he asked.

"Starved," she admitted, locking the door behind her after one last glance at Elvis, who was chowing down on her dinner.

"You worked through lunch again, didn't you?"

"Fifteen days until Christmas," she reminded him.

"I'll take that as a yes," he said, linking their hands as they made their way to his truck. "Do you like pasta?"

"Almost as much as pizza."

Sullivan grinned. "Me, too."

He opened the passenger-side door and helped her into the vehicle before walking around to the driver's side and settling behind the wheel.

"Were you late for work this morning?" she asked, as he drove toward Pastabilities, a popular Italian restaurant in Bronco Heights.

"Not too late," he said. "And Crosby knew that I might be."

"He knows you spent the night in town with me?"

"What he knows—because I was very clear about it this morning—is that we both spent the night at your store, so you don't need to worry about your reputation."

"Darn," she said, only half-joking. "I was hoping some salacious rumors might tarnish my reputation a little."

"You don't like being 'Sweet Sadie' Chamberlin?" he asked, proving that the nickname she'd been given during her adolescence was still in circulation.

Not that she'd never colored outside the lines, but compared to her sister—Do Anything Dana— Sadie had been a saint.

"I just wish that people would realize I'm more than that."

"You're a lot more," Sullivan agreed. "And if the men in this town can't see it, that's their loss—and my gain."

"I imagine any number of them wish they could have spent last night sleeping on the floor of Holiday House," she said dryly.

He shot her a look that she felt to her toes. "I didn't want to be anywhere else."

"Except somewhere with a bed." Heat flooded her cheeks as she realized how he might interpret her words—and that, perhaps, it was precisely how she'd meant them.

"It would have been nice to spend the night in a bed with you," he agreed, holding her gaze. "It would be even better to spend a lot of nights in a bed with you. But…"

She sighed. "There's always a but."

"But my life is in turmoil right now," he reminded her, as he pulled into a vacant parking spot outside the restaurant. "I don't know where I'm going to be in three weeks, never mind three months or three years."

"But it's most likely going to be Columbus," she acknowledged. "Where your parents and your job and your condo are."

"A few days ago, I couldn't have imagined living anywhere else. But now…" He shifted into Park and turned to give her his full attention. "Now I'm open to exploring other possibilities."

Yet another *but*—only this one filled her heart with tentative hope.

Her stomach, however, was still empty, and rumbled an audible reminder of the fact.

Sullivan grinned. "Or maybe now we should focus on getting you fed."

I'm open to exploring other possibilities.

The words echoed in Sullivan's mind the next day as he opened bales of hay and spread the feed over the snow for the cattle.

What did the words even mean?

And what had he been thinking when he'd said them to Sadie?

Maybe that was the problem. Maybe he hadn't been thinking at all. Because being around Sadie seemed to interfere with his thought processes. When he was with her, all he could think about was how pretty she looked, how good she smelled, how much he wanted to kiss her. How much he wanted to do a lot more than kiss her.

Sleeping beside her two nights ago had been torture. Every hormone in his body had been on high alert, painfully aware of her nearness—making him ache to touch her, even knowing that he couldn't. Except that he had been touching her. In fact, their bodies had been pressed close together, from shoulder to thigh. Agonizingly close together.

To preserve body heat, she'd said.

His concern had been *over*heating, because while she'd slept, he'd burned for her.

Maybe he was a jerk for lusting after his brother's former sister-in-law, but he couldn't deny that he did.

Sullivan might have sought her out as a source of information about his twin, but the more time he spent with Sadie, the more he realized he enjoyed being with her.

And when he was with her, he didn't want to be anywhere else.

Obviously, he needed to take a step back. To clear his head. So when Crosby mentioned that some buddies were getting together at Doug's that night, he impulsively accepted the invitation to join them.

When they arrived at the hole-in-the-wall establishment, Sullivan noted that the stools at the bar were all occupied—except for the one roped off with yellow caution tape. The Death Seat was rumored to bring bad luck to anyone who dared sit in it, which Bobby had apparently done only days before his hiking accident.

No wonder the stool remained empty.

He followed Crosby to a high-top table where two other men were filling glasses from a pitcher of beer.

"Just in time to avoid buying a round, I see," a broad-shouldered guy with a red beard said.

"Shut up and pour another glass, JJ," Crosby said.

"You want in on this?" the man named JJ asked Sullivan.

He shook his head. "I'm the designated driver to-night."

"Coke?" the other guy—taller and leaner—asked him.

"Sure."

He snagged a passing server to ask for a soda, then offered his hand across the table as he introduced him-self. "Dale Dalton."

"Sullivan Grainger."

"JJ Mack," the first guy said, completing the intro-ductions.

A pretty server in a low-cut top and short skirt brought Sullivan's soda to the table, then immediately turned her attention to flirting with Crosby.

"When your last name is Abernathy, women can't seem to resist throwing themselves at you," JJ ex-plained to Sullivan when the woman had finally moved on.

Crosby smirked. "How would you know?"

"Because I see it every time I'm here with you," his friend retorted.

"The women do seem to think he's a hot commodity," Dale confirmed. "Even more so now that Wes and Garrett are both off the market."

"The Abernathy bachelor is an endangered species," Crosby acknowledged. "I'm one of the remaining few of a dying breed."

"Don't say that too loud," JJ cautioned. "Or you'll have a lineup of females wanting to perform CPR."

Sullivan sipped his soda. "I'm getting the impression that you guys are all regulars here."

"That surprises you?" Crosby asked.

He shrugged. "I just would have thought The Association would be more your scene," he said, referring to the local—and very exclusive—cattleman's club of which all of the town's wealthiest ranchers were members.

"They have better scotch at The Association," Crosby said. "But you can't really let loose there."

"What he means to say is that, at The Association, you can't be sure the woman you're hitting on isn't someone else's wife," Dale said.

JJ slapped his thigh and guffawed, as if that was the funniest thing he'd ever heard.

"*Once*," Crosby protested. "That happened *once*."

"Once where you got caught, anyway," Dale teased.

"Nothing happened," Crosby said to Sullivan.

He shrugged. "I know it wasn't my wife, because I'm not married."

"You're one of the smart ones then, like us," Dale said approvingly.

"Are we smart?" JJ wondered. "Or just unlucky in love?"

"Pour him another beer before he starts getting philosophical," Crosby said.

Sullivan chuckled, enjoying the easy camaraderie between Crosby's friends. It was something he'd missed since his arrival in Bronco, because he'd been determined to keep to himself, too angry at the world to let anyone in.

Until Sadie.

No. He wasn't going to think about her tonight. Wasn't that the whole point of being here with the guys? To give himself some time and space to get his head on straight.

By the time a second pitcher of beer had been delivered to the table, several other women had stopped by to chat and flirt with Crosby and his buddies. One or two had even sent beckoning glances in his direction, but Sullivan didn't look back.

He might have missed the camaraderie of hanging out with friends, but he hadn't missed hooking up with women he didn't know.

Maybe he was too old for that crap.

Or maybe he was simply too enamored of a specific shopkeeper with long blonde hair and warm brown eyes.

He blinked as JJ snapped his fingers in front of his face. "What?"

The other man laughed. "Where'd you go?"

He shook his head. "It doesn't matter."

"I know where he went," Crosby said. "To Sadie's Holiday House."

"Why would you wanna go there?" Dale asked.

"He's got a thing for Sadie Chamberlin," Crosby answered before Sullivan could.

"Sweet Sadie?" Dale said, sounding surprised.

"She's a nice lady," JJ said, a note of warning in his tone. "Not the type to hook up with a cowboy passing through town."

"I know," Sullivan agreed.

"So why are you wasting your time with her?" Dale wanted to know.

"How is it a waste of time if I enjoy being with her?" he challenged.

"Oh, man." JJ shook his head. "You've got it bad."

Sullivan was afraid the cowboy might be right, but he had no intention of admitting it to these men.

"Are we here to play pool or talk about women?" he asked instead.

"We can do both," Crosby assured him.

And they spent the next few hours doing just that.

Though he knew it was late when he finally got back to his cabin at the Flying A, he pulled out his phone and sent a text message to Sadie.

Crosby dragged me out to Doug's tonight.

He didn't expect a reply.

In fact, he hoped she *didn't* reply, because surely she

would have gone to bed a long time ago. And if she replied, it meant that his message had awakened her.

Why had he even texted her?

Because he'd been thinking about her, missing her, and he couldn't even claim it was a drunk text because he'd had nothing to drink but soda all night.

He'd started to set his phone down when three little dots popped up, indicating that Sadie was tapping a reply.

He should feel guilty for disturbing her. Instead, he found himself grinning as he waited for her response.

Did you have a good time?

I did. But I missed you.

Yep, he actually typed those words.
And sent them.

I stayed late at the store, working on some wreaths. In fact, I just got home a little while ago myself. (But I did sneak home earlier to feed Elvis.)

He shook his head. No wonder the woman had fainted the first time she saw him—she worked herself to the bone.

You worked late tonight and you'll be back again early in the morning, won't you?

Actually, I'm having breakfast with my mom tomorrow, so Beth is opening the shop.

That was unexpected.

Everything okay with your mom?

I hope so.

He wasn't sure what to make of that comment until it was followed by a more detailed response.

Tomorrow is the third anniversary of Dana's death.

He winced.

I'm sorry. That's going to be hard for both of you.

I'm hoping it will get easier with time. But yeah, tomorrow's going to be tough.

Anything I can do to help?

No. But thanks. And thanks for reaching out tonight. It was nice to hear from you.

He didn't know what else to say after that, so he signed off with:

Have a good night.

You, too. xo

And didn't that "xo" have a silly grin spreading across his face again.

JJ was right. He did have it bad.

Chapter Twelve

Roberta held on longer and tighter than usual when Sadie greeted her with a hug the next morning. Yeah, it was going to be a tough day for both of them, but hopefully it would be made a little easier by spending some of it together.

Sadie mourned not only her sister's death but the way she'd lived the last few years of her life. She hadn't really been surprised to learn that Dana had been killed in a drunk driving accident. She *had* been surprised to discover that her sister hadn't been the one driving.

But really, the how and why didn't matter so much as the fact that she was gone. And while Sadie missed her sister every day, she knew Roberta mourned the loss of her child every minute.

"I want to stop at The Watering Can," Roberta said,

as she buckled herself into the passenger seat of Sadie's SUV.

"I thought you might."

Their original plan had been to have breakfast and then go to the cemetery, but her mom had apparently changed her mind and Sadie wasn't going to argue with her.

Instead, she drove directly to the local florist. Roberta had ordered a bouquet of dark purple calla lilies. They'd been Dana's favorite flower—striking and sexy, just like Dana. (Sadie was fond of sunny gerberas—ordinary and plentiful.)

At the cemetery, Sadie stood close to her mom, her arm across her shoulders, attempting to provide both emotional support and a physical barrier against the biting cold. Although both women had dressed appropriately for Montana in December, the subzero temperatures and frigid wind gusts dissuaded them from lingering.

"I'm trying to hold back my tears," Roberta confided in a shaky voice. "Because I'm afraid if I cry, they'll freeze on my face."

Sadie laughed softly. "They probably would."

"I can almost hear your sister chastising us for standing here in the cold, letting our feet go numb."

"Dana was never much for rituals."

"But this is important," Roberta said. "To show that we remember."

"You don't have to prove anything to me," Sadie told her. "I know you miss her every day."

Her mother nodded, stifling a sob.

"So why don't we go somewhere warm and remember happier times?" she suggested.

Roberta nodded again.

And that's what they did. Over plates of Belgian waffles piled high with strawberries and whipped cream—one of Dana's favorite indulgences—they shared their fondest memories, crying a little and laughing a lot.

"I'm not sure I'll ever stop grieving the daughter I lost," her mother confided. "But I'm always grateful, too, for the wonderful daughter I still have."

"Thanks, Mom," Sadie said, sincerely touched by her words.

"So…" Roberta dabbed at her eyes with the corner of her napkin "…tell me what's new with you."

"It's December," she reminded her mother. "Which means that the shop is crazy busy—and so am I."

"I'm glad you love your work, but I worry that you're going to burn out. It seems as if every year, the shop's hours get longer and you work harder."

"Beth and Lynda do a lot, too," Sadie pointed out. "And I hired two students for the holiday season this year."

"I guess the shop must be doing well, if you can afford to pay all those people."

"It's doing very well," she confirmed. "And while we have a lot of regular customers, we're also seeing more people from out of town. People who have heard about the shop and want to check it out. And very few leave empty-handed."

"That's good then," Roberta said, though she didn't sound very convinced.

"And what's new with you?" Sadie asked, turning the tables.

"Nothing's new with me. But my friend Hazel had some exciting news—her daughter-in-law is finally expecting. Twins."

"Good for her," she said, because she knew that was the expected response. What she really wanted to say was "good luck to her," because as much as Sadie loved babies—and she did—she hoped that if and when she ever had a family, the babies came one at a time.

"Hazel is absolutely thrilled," Roberta continued. "You'd think these would be grandbabies one and two, but she's already got four."

Those being the snowplow driver's kids, Sadie knew, though she refrained from commenting in case her mom tried to set her up—once again—with Hazel's twice-divorced son.

Roberta sighed. "Of course, I'm still waiting for my first grandbaby, and hoping it will happen while I'm still around to cuddle him or her."

"I hope so, too, Mom," Sadie said. "But I'd like to fall in love and get married before I make you a grandmother."

"But how are you ever going to meet anyone if you spend every waking hour at work?"

"I meet lots of people every day at the shop."

"How many of them are eligible bachelors?" her mom challenged.

"I can't give you an exact number, but Mr. Howard was flirting with me in the shop the other day."

"Mr. Howard has to be at least seventy years old," Roberta noted dismissively.

"Seventy-two," Sadie confirmed.

Her mother gave her a quizzical glance.

"He told me. But he's still got a full head of hair and all of his own teeth."

"Did he tell you that, too?" Roberta asked her.

"As a matter of fact, he did. He said he wanted me to know that he had more to offer than his old age pension."

Her mother exhaled a long-suffering sigh. "You should talk to your friend Everlee about introducing you to one of her soon-to-be brothers-in-law or the Abernathy cousins."

"Most of Wes's brothers are married or engaged."

"What about the cousins?"

"I've lived in Bronco my whole life. I don't need to be introduced to them—I know who they are. And if anything was going to happen between me and any of the Abernathys or Taylors or Daltons, it would have happened a long time ago."

"Everlee grew up in Bronco, too," Roberta pointed out. "But she and Weston only fell in love recently."

"Will you drop this, Mom? Please?" It wasn't only Sadie's tone that was weary she was tired of having the same conversation with her mother over and over again.

"I just don't understand why you're so opposed to meeting someone."

"I'm not opposed to meeting anyone. In fact, I'd love

to meet someone, and I'm still optimistic that it will happen for me someday"

Even if she'd begun to suspect that her long hours weren't an impediment to that goal but rather a deliberate effort to fill time she would otherwise spend alone. Because at least at the shop, she had customers to interact with or Beth or Lynda to talk to.

"But right now, I'd like to talk about something else," she said firmly.

Roberta smiled her thanks to the server who refilled her coffee. She took her time emptying two creamers and two packets of sugar into her mug, then stirred.

"Have you seen any more of… Bobby's brother?" she finally asked.

"His name's Sullivan," Sadie reminded her mother. "And yes, I've seen him a few times."

Because what was the point in denying it? No doubt someone who knew her mom had seen her and Sullivan together—or seen his truck parked in her driveway—and reported back to her.

"Is there something going on there?" Roberta wondered.

Maybe. Hopefully.

"We're friends," she said. Not just an answer to the question but also a reminder to herself.

Friends who'd shared a couple of really steamy kisses, but so far, nothing more than that—and definitely nothing that she wanted to share with her mother.

It was almost one o'clock by the time Sadie arrived at her shop after dropping Roberta back at her apartment. As she breathed in the familiar scents of spiced apple cider and warm gingerbread, she felt some of the tension seeping out of her muscles.

Beth finished checking out a trio of customers and wished each one a "Merry Christmas" as she passed their purchases across the counter. When the three women had gone, she came out from behind the counter and wrapped her arms around Sadie.

"Dammit," Sadie muttered, as her throat tightened up and tears stung her eyes.

Her friend immediately pulled back. "Did I do something wrong?"

"No." Sadie sniffled. "I just didn't realize how much I needed a hug until that moment."

Beth embraced her again. "We all need hugs sometimes—and I figured that today is definitely one of those times for you."

"Because it's the anniversary of my sister's death or because I spent the last three and a half hours with my mom?"

"Maybe both?"

Sadie managed a laugh. "Thanks, pal."

"Seriously—how are you doing?"

"I'm okay."

"Are you sure? Because Noah and I can handle things here if you want to take the rest of the day off."

"I appreciate it," Sadie said. "But I think I'll feel better if I keep busy."

"In that case, I should probably tell you that Mrs. Beckett came in this morning to order two custom wreaths—one for each of her daughters."

"When does she need them by?"

"Friday."

Sadie winced.

"I told her it was an unreasonable request," Beth said. "But she's apparently leaving for Oregon on Saturday to spend part of the holidays with each of them and she wants to take them with her."

"Then I guess I better look at the paperwork and ensure I've got all the materials I need."

"So you are going to do them?"

"She's one of our best customers," Sadie reminded her friend. "I wouldn't want to disappoint her."

"I figured you'd say that, which is why I told her that there would be a twenty percent premium added to the usual price for rush service."

She gasped. "You didn't."

"I did," Beth said unapologetically. "And she didn't even blink."

"She's willing to pay an extra twenty percent—and she didn't blink?"

"Most businesses charge extra for expedited service," her colleague pointed out. "Why shouldn't we do the same?"

"Weren't you concerned that she might decide to take her business elsewhere?"

"Where else would she take it? No one does work like you do. Why do you think she comes from Bronco Heights to shop here?"

"You really do have a good head for business," Sadie noted.

FREE BOOKS GIVEAWAY

2 FREE ROMANCE BOOKS!

2 FREE WHOLESOME ROMANCE BOOKS!

GET UP TO FOUR FREE BOOKS & TWO FREE GIFTS WORTH OVER $20!

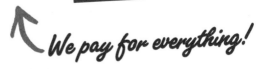

We pay for everything!

See Details Inside

Complete the survey below and return it today to receive up to 4 FREE BOOKS and FREE GIFTS guaranteed!

"It's basic supply and demand," Beth said. "Economics one-oh-one."

"Maybe in the New Year we should talk about a partnership."

The other woman sucked in a breath. "Do you mean it?"

"Is it something you'd be interested in?" Sadie asked her.

"Absolutely."

"Then let's put it on the schedule. And if you and Noah have things under control here, I'll get started on those wreaths."

It was a short journey from the flower shop to Sadie's Holiday House—and a fraction of the distance he'd traveled from the ranch after work—but Sullivan spent the entire five-minute drive second-guessing his impulsive purchase. And questioning his choice as he struggled to get the pot through the door.

"I'm sorry, sir." The words were spoken by a woman hanging stockings on a row of hooks behind the cash register. "No pets except service animals and no plants except medicinal herbs."

He shifted the pot to one side so that he wasn't looking at her through a forest of red petals. "Is that a joke?"

She smiled. "Yes, it's a joke."

"Oh." He smiled back, feeling foolish. "I'm looking for Sadie."

"And you would be...?"

"Sullivan Grainger."

"Is she expecting you?"

"No," he admitted. "This is an impromptu visit." He gestured to the plant. "And a questionable decision."

She laughed. "Sadie's upstairs in the craft room. I'll show you the way."

He followed her up the staircase and down a hall, where she paused to knock on a partially open door.

"Sadie, you've got a visitor," she said, then stepped aside so that he could enter.

"Sullivan," Sadie said, obviously surprised to see him.

He set the plant on the table in front of her.

"What's this?" she asked.

"I don't know a lot about flowers, but the woman at the flower shop said it was a poinsettia. Apparently, it's the December birth flower, said to bring wishes of mirth and celebration."

Sadie rolled her eyes. "I know what a poinsettia is—although I didn't know the mirth and celebration part," she admitted. "Perhaps what I should have asked is, *why* did you bring me a poinsettia?"

He shrugged. "I thought it would add a little holiday spirit to your house."

She laughed. "You thought my house was lacking something, did you?"

"And there it is," he said.

"What?"

"The sparkle that was missing from your eyes."

Once again, her throat grew tight. Because while Sullivan was tiptoeing around the subject more than Beth had done, she knew the real reason he'd brought the plant was to brighten her mood on a dark day.

"Thank you for the poinsettia," she said. "It's beautiful. And enormous."

"When it comes to Christmas stuff, your motto seems to be Go Big or Go Home."

She laughed again. "Well, you certainly went big."

"I'm just glad that you were here," he told her. "Because it was awkward enough carrying that thing in here—I didn't want to have to drag it out again."

"I'm sure," she agreed. "But what are you doing in town? Because I certainly hope you didn't come all this way to bring me a poinsettia."

"It's not that far," he said. "And it's not the only reason I came to town. I was also hoping to convince you to play hooky for half an hour."

Sadie looked at the ribbons and pinecones and baubles spread out on the table. "I've got a lot of work to do here. And if I'm not working here, I should be working downstairs. Beth and Noah have been handling the customers all day."

"And doing a fine job of it, as far as I could tell."

"I know they are," she agreed. "But I wouldn't feel right skipping out on them again."

"Come with me," he said.

She hesitated about half a second before walking around the table to take his proffered hand.

He led her down the stairs, to the main showroom where Beth was now rearranging ornaments and Noah was wrapping packages.

"Do you guys mind if I steal Sadie away for thirty minutes?"

"Why are you asking us?" Noah said. "Sadie's the boss."

"We don't mind," Beth said. "Take all the time you need."

Sullivan turned to Sadie again.

She sighed. "Okay, you've got thirty minutes."

"You're going to want to bundle up. It's cold outside."

She donned her outerwear and they exited the shop.

"Where are we going?" she asked.

"Nowhere in particular."

"You don't strike me as the type of guy to wander aimlessly," she remarked.

"Not having a destination isn't the same thing as not having a purpose."

"Okay, *why* are we going nowhere in particular?"

"Because, over the past couple of weeks, I think I've started to realize how much you love the Christmas season. But I've also realized that you're so busy helping other people—whether it's choosing an appropriate garland for a reclaimed barn-wood mantel or settling on a decorating theme for a blended family's first Christmas together or finding the perfect gift for Great Aunt Edna—"

"Apparently, you've been paying attention when you've been in Holiday House," she mused.

"You're so busy helping other people," he said again, ignoring her interruption, "that you don't take time to look around and appreciate all the ways your friends and neighbors embrace and celebrate the season."

"So we're taking a walk to look at other people's Christmas decorations?" she asked dubiously.

"We're taking a walk to enjoy the Christmas spirit that's all around." He tucked her mittened hand in the crook of his arm. "And just being together."

"I can't object to that," Sadie said.

So they wandered through town, admiring the lights twinkling along rooflines and evergreen garlands draped on porches and lopsided snowmen wearing floppy hats and knitted scarves. And maybe Sadie still didn't really understand why Sullivan had insisted on dragging her away from the shop, but she nevertheless enjoyed being with him. Even if she had to continually remind herself that they were just friends, because walking hand-in-hand with him made her wish that they could be more.

Then it started to snow—big, fluffy flakes that danced and swirled and wrapped the peaceful evening in magic.

"Thank you for this," she said, tipping her head against Sullivan's shoulder.

"Are you honestly thanking me for dragging you outside for a leisurely stroll in minus-ten-degree weather?"

"I'm thanking you for making me take the time to look at and appreciate the world around me," she clarified.

"It was my pleasure," he said.

"But as much fun as this has been, we should probably head back before we both get frostbite."

"How about some hot cocoa before we return to the real world?"

"Mmm, hot cocoa sounds yummy," she said. "But Bean & Biscotti closes early on Mondays."

"Isn't there a diner at the end of this block?"

"There is," she confirmed, dragging her feet a little as she followed him in that direction.

"I bet we could get hot cocoa there."

"We could, but…"

"There's always a but," he said, echoing her words from a few days earlier.

"But…it's where my mom works."

"And you don't want to have to make introductions?" he guessed, pausing on the sidewalk outside the diner.

"Do you want to meet my mother?" she asked, her tone dubious.

He shrugged. "Her daughter's pretty cool, so I can't imagine she's so terrifying."

Still, it required some effort on Sadie's part to shove aside her concerns and put a smile on her face. "In that case, let's go get ourselves some hot cocoa."

The bell jingled over the door when Sullivan pulled it open and gestured for her to enter.

She breathed a silent sigh of relief when she saw Alice Hutchinson behind the counter and no sign of her mom. Maybe Roberta had finished early tonight or maybe she was in the kitchen. Either way, Sadie was optimistic that she and Sullivan could be in and out without crossing her path.

She made her way directly to the counter, but instead of settling onto one of the vacant stools, she remained standing as she returned Alice's friendly greeting and asked for two hot cocoas "to go."

"You don't want to sit here for a few minutes to let your toes thaw?" Sullivan asked.

"We've already been out longer than the half hour I told Beth and Noah I'd be gone," she pointed out.

He shrugged and pulled out his wallet to pay for their beverages.

Alice smiled her thanks when Sullivan waved away the change she offered to him, and Sadie breathed another sigh as she turned away from the counter with her hot drink in hand.

Too soon, she realized, as her mother's voice sounded behind her.

"Aren't you going to introduce me to…your friend?"

Chapter Thirteen

"You took Sullivan to meet *your mother*?" Evy's jaw almost hit the table. She was sitting with Sadie, enjoying an early morning caffeine boost in Bean & Biscotti before opening their respective shops. "That's a big step."

"It wasn't a step," Sadie denied, wrapping her hands around her cappuccino. "It was…a crossing of paths. An awkward crossing."

Evy licked foamed milk from the rim of her cup. "Do you think it was hard for your mom, that he looks so much like Bobby?"

"No doubt that was part of it."

"And the other part?" her friend prompted.

"I think my mom might have sensed that there's something between me and Sullivan," she confided.

"Why would that be a problem? Hasn't she been trying to set you up with every single man she knows—*and* his brother?"

"She has," Sadie confirmed. "But I don't think she's keen on the idea of me dating *Bobby's* brother."

"Is that what's happening? Are you and Sullivan…" Evy paused deliberately "…dating?"

She shrugged. "I don't really know. We've had one date. At least, when he took me to Pastabilities he said it was a date. Mostly, we just hang out.

"But he comes into town frequently to see me," she noted. "And I like to think that means something."

"It definitely means something," Evy agreed. "And anyone who's seen the way he looks at you would know that he has feelings for you."

"And yet…he hasn't done anything more than kiss me. And I'm not complaining about the kissing, because it's…amazing. I just thought he'd be wanting more. Dammit," Sadie said. "*I* want more."

"You know, there's no rule that says a woman has to wait for a man to make all the moves," her friend told her. "And even if there was, I'd advocate breaking it."

"I've thought about it, but then I wonder what might be holding him back—and I think I know what it might be."

"Trying to read a man's mind is never a good idea."

"He's a good guy," Sadie continued, ignoring the warning. "And he knows that I have abandonment issues, and I think he's decided not to get any more deeply involved because he doesn't want me to be hurt when he leaves. Because he *is* going to leave, Evy."

"So far, the man hasn't given any indication that he's going anywhere," her friend pointed out. "He's even got a job in Bronco now."

"A temporary job," Sadie reminded Evy—and herself.

Because it was important that she not get her hopes up. Not let herself be disappointed. *Again*.

"Anyway, that's enough about me," she decided. "Tell me what's going on with your wedding plans."

So they spent the next twenty minutes chatting about Evy's ideas for flowers and cakes and dresses—which were apparently very different from her daughter's ideas. And four-year-old Lola was known to have strong opinions—and to express them loudly.

"So she's going to be the flower girl—which is what I wanted, too. And Archie's going to be the ring bearer—which I have some concerns about."

"Understandable," Sadie said. Because she'd met Archie—he was adorable and eager to please, but he was also a puppy, and puppies were unpredictable.

"Lola's promised to hold tight to his leash and watch over him all day, but the real kicker was when she said that Archie has to be part of the big day because he saved Wes's life, and the only reason we're getting to marry Wes is that he's not dead."

"It's scary the way that child's mind works at her age." But from what Sadie had heard, the little girl wasn't wrong—the pup had inserted himself between Wes and an angry mama bear and been rewarded with a swipe of an enormous paw. It was only thanks to prompt veterinary attention that the dog had survived and made a complete recovery.

"Wes said she's either going to be in college or prison by the time she's twelve."

Sadie laughed. "He did not."

"He did," Evy insisted. "But he also agreed with Lola's logic about including the dog in our wedding."

"That is something I can't wait to see."

"You'll have a front row seat," her friend promised.

"I think you're going to need another shopping basket," a familiar voice remarked to Sullivan as he surveyed the various packages of minilights on the shelf at Sadie's Holiday House.

He turned to give the proprietor a smile. "I think you're right," he agreed. "I also need some advice."

"About what?" Sadie asked.

"Clear lights or colored? And how many strands?"

"You're getting a Christmas tree?" she guessed.

He nodded. "While we were out walking the other night, counting inflatable Santas and animatronic reindeer, it occurred to me that I haven't decorated my cabin and it could definitely use some festive touches."

"So you're planning to do more than put up a tree?"

He winked. "Go Big or Go Home, right?"

"I've created a monster," she said, but immediately followed the remark with a grin.

"So…lights?" he prompted.

"Clear or colored is really a matter of personal preference," she told him.

"I like the traditional red, green, yellow and blue."

It was what was familiar to him—what his mom and dad had always strung on their tree.

"Then you want these," Sadie said, selecting a package from the shelf. "How big is your tree?"

"I have no idea, because I haven't got it yet, but Crosby said I could chop one down on the ranch."

"That sounds like fun," she said.

Sullivan drew back. "What do you mean *sounds like fun*?"

"Just that I've never actually done that before," Sadie confided.

"You—who claims to be an expert on all things Christmas?" he asked incredulously.

"I don't claim to be an expert but an enthusiast."

"Well, you should definitely cut down your own tree at least once," he told her. "And since I know how to cut down a tree but not much about decorating, maybe you could come out to the ranch and we could do both together?"

"I'd like that."

"Great," he said, struggling to hold back a grin and not entirely sure he'd succeeded. "But I still have no idea how many strings of lights I'm going to need."

"The general rule of thumb is one strand of lights per foot of tree, but it's really personal preference— do you want a really bright tree or a less bright one?"

"Go Big or Go Home," he said again, tossing several more packages of lights on top of a basket already overflowing with ornaments.

The lights slid off the pile and onto the floor.

With a shake of her head, Sadie walked away.

"Not that I don't appreciate the business," she said when she'd returned with a second basket into which she transferred the lights. "But I feel compelled to tell you that you could get some of this stuff cheaper if you went to one of the big stores in the city."

"I believe in supporting local businesses."

"An admirable perspective," she said. "I just don't know if you realize how much all of this is going to cost. And you're not done yet."

"What am I missing?"

"A tree topper."

"And that's why I came here," he said. "Because a clerk at a big-box store wouldn't tell me I needed one of those."

She took him to the display of tree toppers. There were angels and stars and snowflakes and fancy bows and—

"Hey, can I put Darth Vader on top of my tree?"

"You can put whatever you want on top of your tree—even Sponge Bob, if you want your visitors to think it was decorated by an eight-year-old."

"You're not impressed with the Darth Vader?"

"A topper like that works better if the theme is carried through all the trimmings—TIE fighter lights and character ornaments."

"You have TIE fighter lights?"

"Sorry. Sold out."

His gaze narrowed. "I don't think you're being entirely truthful with me."

"I thought you wanted a more traditional Christmas tree."

"I do. But a Star Wars tree would be cool," he said just a little wistfully.

In the end, he decided on a tin snowflake topper, which Sadie assured him was both traditional and contemporary and perfectly suitable.

"When did you plan on cutting down your tree?" Sadie asked, as she scanned his purchases.

"If you're available tonight, I could come back to pick you up at closing."

"There's no need for that," she protested. "I can find my way to the ranch."

He wasn't entirely comfortable with the idea of her having to drive all that way—and back again—on her own, but all he said was, "I'll text you directions to my cabin."

Sadie figured it would be easier to pick out and cut down a tree in the daylight, so she left Lynda in charge of the shop and headed out around four, sending Sullivan a text message to let him know that she was on her way.

Twenty minutes later, as she parked by the picturesque cabin, he came out the front door.

"Hey," he said, greeting her with a smile when she stepped out of her SUV.

She offered him the wreath and wreath hanger she'd retrieved from the back seat. "A cabin-warming gift."

"I didn't think about a wreath, and I should have," he said. "Let me pay you for that."

"If you paid me for it, it wouldn't be a gift, would it?"

"But—"

"Just say 'thank you,' Sullivan."

"Thank you, Sullivan," he parroted.

She rolled her eyes but raised herself on her toes to kiss him lightly.

He hooked the hanger over the door and set the wreath in place.

"Looks like Christmas around here already," Sadie said approvingly.

"It does," Sullivan agreed.

And now that his hands were free, he pulled her close and kissed her again, longer and deeper this time.

"Are you ready to go tree hunting now?" he asked when he'd finally eased his mouth from hers.

"That's why I'm here," she reminded him.

"Okay then," he said. "Let's go find a Christmas tree."

She pulled her hat lower on her head and shoved her hands into her mittens while he picked up the tools he'd already gathered for their excursion.

"What kind of saw is that?" she asked, eyeing the small but wicked-looking teeth on the blade warily.

"A bow saw. It will make quick work of a trunk less than six inches in diameter."

"And what's the rope for?"

"To tie around the tree so it's easier to drag back to the cabin."

"Obviously this isn't your first rodeo," she noted.

He winked. "And not my first tree cutting, either."

They walked hand-in-hand toward a heavily wooded area behind Sullivan's cabin. The snow crunched beneath their boots and their breath made clouds in the pine-scented air, but mostly Sadie was aware of the man beside her and the way his nearness warmed her blood so that she barely registered the cold.

"Now what?" Sadie asked when he paused near a stand of trees.

"Now you pick one you like and cut it down."

It might have been her first time, but she knew what to look for in a tree. Obviously, it needed to be straight, with lots of branches to hold the lights and ornaments.

She gestured to a conifer that seemed to fit the basic requirements. "Can you stand next to that one?"

"Why? Do you want to make sure we'll look good together in pictures?" he teased.

She rolled her eyes. "I'm trying to gauge its height."

Sullivan stood beside the tree.

"It's at least a foot taller than you," she noted. "Probably about seven-and-a-half feet."

"The cabin has ten-foot ceilings, so that will work," he said.

"Then I guess we've found your tree."

He stepped away from it and offered her the saw.

She instinctively took a step back. "Don't give that thing to me."

He chuckled. "Aren't you here because you've never cut down a tree before and you wanted to do so?"

"I wanted to be part of the experience," she said. "I didn't expect to actually have to do the work."

"It's not a lot of work," he promised. "And the saw is a very basic tool."

He showed her how to hold the saw—placing her dominant hand on the handle and her other hand on top of the frame. Then, with his hands guiding hers, he positioned the blade parallel to the ground and showed her how to use it.

"Look at that," she said, as the sharp teeth cut into the trunk. "I'm doing it."

"You're doing a great job," he said, lifting his hands away from hers.

"Wait. Where are you going?"

"I'm just going to stand on the other side, to pull the tree so it doesn't bind the saw."

"Am I supposed to know what that means?"

"Just keep sawing," he told her.

She followed his instructions, and the sharp teeth of the blade made fairly quick work of the trunk.

"I did it," she said when the tree toppled. "I cut down a Christmas tree."

She looked so cute, so proud, that he couldn't resist dropping a kiss on her lips.

"Mmm," she said. "If that's my reward, give me back the saw so I can cut down a dozen more."

He chuckled. "I don't think the Abernathys would appreciate you felling the whole lot, but I welcome your enthusiasm."

"Can I pull the tree back to the cabin?" she asked, determined now to experience every stage of the tree-cutting process.

"It's going to be heavy," he warned, as he looped the rope around the trunk.

"I'm stronger than I look," Sadie told him.

He handed her the rope.

She tugged.

"And it's heavier than it looks," she admitted, feeling the strain in her arms though the tree wasn't budging.

He took the other end of the rope and added his muscle to the task, and they dragged the tree back to his cabin together.

Chapter Fourteen

Wrangling the tree through the front door of his cabin was another challenge, but eventually they succeeded, and with most of the needles still attached.

"Whew!" Sadie tugged off her mittens and hat and unzipped her coat. "You really do that every year?"

"I'm surprised that you don't." Sullivan removed his coat and boots, too. "There must be plenty of places around here where you can cut down your own tree."

"But what happens when you get caught?"

He chuckled. "I was referring to Christmas tree farms."

"I guess there are," she agreed. "Though most people I know who have real trees get them already cut and wrapped."

"I'm not sure that even counts as a real tree."

"I'm not getting into that debate with you," Sadie decided. "Tell me what we do next."

"Are you hungry?"

"Now that you mention it."

"I picked up a tray of penne with sausage and peppers from Pastabilities when I was in town today. Why don't I throw that in the oven to heat while we're getting the tree set up?"

"Sounds good to me."

Wrestling the tree into the stand really was a two-person job, and he was grateful that Sadie was there to help. And pleased that he'd suggested he would hold the tree, since he was taller, while she stretched out on the floor beneath the lowest branches to guide the trunk into position, because it gave him a prime view of her nicely rounded bottom, encased today in faded denim.

It was the first time he'd seen her in jeans, he realized. Usually she wore skirts—long and flowy—that looked really good on her, too. But he could only imagine what her legs looked like beneath the skirts, while the snug-fitting denim provided his imagination with much more detail. And he definitely liked what he saw.

Of course, he liked everything about Sadie. Her eyes. Her smile. Her warmth. Her laughter. Her—

"Am I done here?" she asked, interrupting his musing.

"Oh, yeah," he said. "That's great."

She wiggled out from under the tree, and he discovered he liked the way she wiggled, too.

"What?" she asked suspiciously. "Why are you smiling?"

"Am I?" He reached out to pluck a pine needle from her hair. Then one caught in the knit of her sweater. And another.

"I probably have more needles on me than the tree."

"Not even close," he said, drawing her into his arms and turning her around so that she was facing the tree. "What do you think?"

"I think I picked a pretty good tree."

"I think you did, too."

She did a half circle in his embrace, so that they were face-to-face now. "I'm glad you invited me to help."

"And I'm really glad you're here."

And because he couldn't resist, he kissed her again.

And she kissed him back with a passion and enthusiasm that were so typical of Sadie, he had to wonder what was wrong with the men in Bronco that none of them had snapped her up. He was equally baffled by the high school boyfriend and almost-fiancé who'd been foolish enough to ever walk away from her.

But just when things were starting to get interesting, the oven timer buzzed.

Damn.

"Pasta's ready."

"I guess we'd better wash up for dinner."

He wanted to suggest an alternative plan —one that postponed food in favor of getting naked. But as much as he wanted Sadie—and he was long past the stage of being able to deny that he wanted her—he was wary of taking their relationship to the next step when so much about his life was still unsettled.

Though he was finally taking steps toward changing that.

"You were busy in town today," Sadie noted, as she dug into the plate of pasta he'd served up for her. "Buying out half the inventory at Holiday House and bringing home half the menu at Pastabilities."

"I think you're exaggerating just a little," he said.

"Really?" she challenged, gesturing to the penne, parmesan garlic breadsticks, salad and antipasto spread out on the table.

"It's hardly half the menu," he said, the protest followed by a sheepish grin before he circled back to her original comment. "But you're right—I was busy today. I even made a stop at Town Hall."

Sadie reached for a breadstick. "What were you doing at Town Hall?"

"A search of birth records, as you suggested."

"Did you have any luck?" she asked cautiously.

He nodded. "Clayton Stone and Delilah Smith were married in Bronco on September 30, 1961 and they had three children—a daughter named Michelle, then another daughter, Aubrey, followed by a son, Oliver, who died before his first birthday.

"Following up on that, I looked for birth records listing either Michelle or Aubrey as the mother—hoping that one of the sisters might have been Bobby's. And sure enough, I found his birth registration—along with the registration for another baby, also born to Aubrey Stone on the same date, identified only as 'Baby Boy Stone.'"

Sadie gasped. "That's your original birth registration?"

He nodded again. "So it appears that my brother was raised by our biological family...but I was not."

And that raised more questions for him than it answered.

No doubt it was a common refrain of adopted children—why didn't my birth parents want me? And, logically, Sullivan understood that it sometimes wasn't a case of the parents not wanting their baby but wanting a better life for him or her. And he'd been given that when he was adopted by Louis and Ellie Grainger.

Still, he was baffled by the realization that his birth mother had chosen to raise one of her twins and not the other.

Why had she kept Bobby but given Sullivan away?

"Were you able to find anything else out about your...about Aubrey?" Sadie asked.

Now he shook his head. "It's as if she completely disappeared."

"So what's your next step?"

"I'm going to see Michelle and hope that she can answer some of my questions," he said. "I was worried I might discover that she'd moved across the country—or even out of the country—but a quick Google search revealed that she lives in Rust Creek Falls."

"That trip shouldn't take you very long."

"I should be there and back in a day. Depending on how much, if anything, Michelle is willing to say."

"When are you going?"

"Tomorrow."

"When you decide to do something, you don't waste any time, do you?"

"I feel as if enough time has been wasted."

"I wish I could go with you," she said.

"I'm grateful you'd even think of offering, but I understand that this is a busy time of year for you at the shop. And honestly, I think this is something I need to do on my own." He offered a wry smile. "Or maybe I'm not sure I want anyone else to know what she might tell me."

"You do know that anything she tells you will say more about your birth mother than you, don't you?"

"Sure," he agreed, though not very convincingly.

"Whatever her reasons for giving you up had nothing to do with you personally," Sadie insisted. "Maybe the idea of caring for two babies was just overwhelming."

"Maybe." He pushed aside his empty plate. "Anyway, that's tomorrow. Tonight, we have a tree to decorate."

And for the next few hours, they focused on doing just that. Or at least tried. But working in close proximity, it was inevitable that their shoulders would bump or their hands would touch, then glances would be exchanged and kisses stolen, savored.

"Last one," Sadie said when she handed him a glossy red ball with a gold bow.

"That's it? We're done?"

"We're done," she confirmed, starting to gather up the empty packages.

"Don't worry about that," he said. "I'll take care of it."

"I'm not going to leave you with all this mess," she protested.

"It won't take me too long to tidy up, and we're already later than I thought we'd be."

"I don't have a curfew, you know," she said, sounding amused.

He drew her into his arms. "I'm not suggesting that you have to go home, just that I don't want to waste time tidying up when there are other things we could be doing."

"I think we've spent a lot of time doing *other things* already tonight," she remarked.

But she didn't protest when he dipped his head to kiss her again. In fact, her lips parted willingly and her tongue danced and dallied with his in a sensual rhythm that made everything inside her tremble and yearn.

And oh, how she yearned for him.

But while her hormones were more than willing to follow wherever he might lead, her brain urged caution, reminding her that she'd been down this road before—and it led straight to heartbreak.

And so, with more than a little regret, Sadie eased her mouth from his.

"I should head home."

She wondered—maybe even hoped—that he might try to change her mind. And another kiss would have been all the persuasion she needed.

But Sullivan took a step back. "Elvis is probably waiting for you," he acknowledged.

She nodded.

"Will you text me when you get home?"

"If you insist."

"I insist." He brushed his lips over hers again—a quick, light kiss this time. "Thank you for helping with my tree."

"Thank you for letting me help. And for dinner. Again."

As she drove away, Sadie couldn't help wishing that he'd asked her to stay.

The drive to Rust Creek Falls seemed to take forever—until Sullivan's GPS announced that he was "arriving at destination." And suddenly he was assailed by doubts.

What was he doing here?

Should he have called first?

What if Michelle refused to talk to him?

What if she pretended not to know anything about him?

What if she *really* didn't know anything about him?

He shifted into Park and dropped his head against the steering wheel.

Maybe he should turn around and drive back to Bronco.

And he might have done so if not for the fact that Sadie would be waiting to hear from him, wanting to know what he learned.

I drove all the way to Rust Creek Falls only to find out that she wasn't there. "On vacation," a neighbor told me.

It wasn't an implausible story, and maybe Sadie would believe it. But he didn't want to lie to her.

What he wanted—what he needed—were answers.

And he'd come too far to go back now.

And if Michelle Stone couldn't or wouldn't provide the information he sought, then he wasn't out anything more than a few hours of time and a tank of gas.

So resolved, he got out of his truck and made his way to the door.

Before he even had a chance to knock, he heard a low growl on the other side.

Apparently, Aunt Michelle had a dog. One that didn't like strangers.

Still, he lifted his hand and knocked.

The growl turned to a bark. Deep and menacing.

He stood his ground and ignored the bead of sweat that was slowly snaking its way down his spine.

He liked dogs. He understood that they were territorial creatures and as long as he didn't pose a threat—and he didn't—there wouldn't be a problem.

"Hush, Oscar," a female voice said firmly.

The dog hushed.

The door opened.

Sullivan had seen the woman's birth registration, so he was prepared to meet an almost sixty-year-old woman. He wasn't prepared to see his own eyes in her face, and whatever words he'd intended to say, stuck in his throat.

"Can I help you?" she asked. Then her eyes grew wide, and she lifted a hand to her mouth. "*Bobby?*"

He quickly shook his head. "No, ma'am. I'm not Bobby Stone. I'm Sullivan Grainger."

Her hand slipped from her mouth to her chest. "You're his brother." Those all-too-familiar eyes filled with tears. "You have to be his brother. The one who was adopted."

"It sounds like you know more about my past than I do," he noted.

"Come on in," she said, stepping away from the door to allow him entry. "And I'll tell you everything I know."

Sadie didn't hear from Sullivan all day.

She checked her cell phone more times than she wanted to admit, to see if he'd sent her a message. And each time, she'd been disappointed.

She thought about reaching out to him, but she didn't want to pressure him. If he learned anything that he wanted to share, he'd reach out to her.

Still, she stayed at the shop a little longer than necessary after closing, because he had a habit of showing up there and she was hopeful that he'd do so. But when seven o'clock became eight, she finally gave up and headed home.

Elvis padded into the hallway when she opened the front door, only to ensure that Sadie saw her flick her tail and walk away.

"I know I'm late," she acknowledged, taking off her boots and coat. "But I came home on my break this afternoon to feed you, so there's no reason for you to be flicking your tail at me."

Elvis was unimpressed with her logic.

"Some people fill their cat's bowl with food in the morning and let them graze all day, but I take time out of my day to come home and feed you. And what do I get in return? Attitude."

And now Sadie was talking to the cat—and giving Elvis attitude right back because directing her frustration toward her feline companion was easier than directing it at Sullivan, whom she hadn't heard from all day.

"I didn't even think about my own dinner." She opened the refrigerator now and examined the meager contents. "I don't even know when I was last at the grocery store, but I know I was at the pet store just a few days ago to stock up on your food and treats."

She selected a container of fruit-at-the-bottom yogurt, checked the date and reasoned that "best before" didn't mean "bad" only four days later.

She was reaching for a spoon when a knock sounded.

Her heart leapt inside her chest, because she felt certain it had to be Sullivan at the door. Because she didn't know anyone else who would just drop by this time of night.

She forgot about the yogurt and hurried down the hall, peeking through the sidelight to confirm the identity of her visitor before letting him in.

It *was* Sullivan—with a pizza box in hand.

"You're back," she said by way of greeting.

"I'm back," he confirmed with a smile, and her heart leapt again. "And I brought food."

"I feel as if I should protest the fact that you always

seem to be feeding me, but I'm almost as happy to see that pizza as I am to see you."

"Obviously you haven't had dinner," he noted.

"I was—"

"Working late," he finished for her.

"Nine days until Christmas," she pointed out, taking the box from him so that he could remove his boots and coat.

"I'm aware."

He was in a good mood, Sadie mused, as she gathered plates and napkins. Which gave her hope that the meeting with his aunt had gone well.

"Do you want a beer or soda?" she asked when he joined her in the kitchen.

"Soda's fine," he said.

She set two cans of Coke on the table.

Elvis, drawn by the sounds of their conversation, and looking for another opportunity to let Sadie know that she was only annoyed with *her*, sauntered toward Sullivan. It had taken a few visits for the cat to warm to him, but now she not only tolerated his presence but occasionally rubbed up against him, encouraging him to reach down and pet her.

Today, however, as soon as she got within a couple of feet of him, Elvis immediately recoiled and backed away.

"Apparently, my cat is giving everyone attitude today," Sadie remarked.

"I bet she smells Oscar on me."

Sadie's brows lifted in a silent question.

"Michelle fosters animals," Sullivan explained, as

he opened the pizza box and gestured for Sadie to help herself before he did the same. "Oscar is a four-year-old lab-shepherd mix that she's taking care of right now."

"Obviously you met your aunt."

He nodded, his mouth full.

"What's she like?"

He swallowed. "She seems really great. Certainly more accommodating than I would have been if some long-lost relative showed up at my door."

"Do you know why she left Bronco?"

He nodded. "She took a temp job in Rust Creek Falls, fell in love, got married and decided to stay.

"I met her husband, Gary, too. He sells real estate, so weekends are busy for him—even nine days before Christmas—and when he came home for lunch, he had some questions about why his wife was crying over old photo albums with a strange man."

"I imagine he would," Sadie acknowledged.

"But she'd obviously shared her family history with him already, because as soon as she introduced me as Bobby's twin brother, he seemed to understand."

"Do you have any cousins through Michelle and Gary?"

He shook his head. "Michelle decided early on that she didn't want any kids of her own, because the women in her family weren't very good mothers, and she didn't want to perpetuate the cycle."

"Meaning her mom and her sister?" Sadie guessed.

"Her grandmother wasn't the warm and fuzzy type, either."

"Was she able to tell you anything about your mom?"

"She told me as much as she knew—and that they'd lost touch years ago. She also gave me photos of… Aubrey. She didn't have any of Ken—my birth father. Said he was trouble with a capital 'T' from day one and had warned her sister repeatedly about him. But Aubrey refused to heed her warnings. He was a few years older with a bad boy reputation, and she was going through a rebellious stage."

"An all-too-familiar tale," Sadie mused.

"So you could probably guess that he took off when she got pregnant, because she was barely sixteen and he was almost twenty. But he didn't get far before he was caught holding up a convenience store and went to jail—not for the first time.

"Apparently, her parents—my grandparents—were the ones who encouraged Aubrey to give up the baby when they learned she was pregnant. They said they were done raising their kids and weren't going to raise hers, and there was no way Aubrey—still a kid herself—could take care of a baby on her own, so she reluctantly agreed.

"According to Michelle, her sister tried to back out of the arrangement after giving birth, but the papers had already been signed and there was a wonderful couple waiting to give her baby a good home.

"And all the paperwork referenced *a* baby— singular—because no one had known that she was pregnant with twins. As it turned out, the second-born infant was so extremely underweight that the doctors didn't expect him to live more than a few days. But Au-

brey's parents—my grandparents—used him as lever-
age, promising that if she gave up her firstborn, they'd
let her keep the second one."

"That's horrible," Sadie said, her heart aching for
the teen mom who'd been set up to lose a second child
after being forced to give up her first. Knowing that
second child was Bobby made Sadie feel even worse.

"But not as bad as it could have been—because
Bobby survived. Not long enough for me to know him,"
Sullivan acknowledged ruefully. "But he beat the odds
and lived."

"How do you feel, now that you know all of this?"
she asked gently.

"I guess I feel…relieved," he finally decided. "Grateful that so many of my questions have finally been answered. Lucky that I was given the opportunity to be
raised by a family who really did love me. And sorry
that Bobby wasn't given the same opportunities."

"I know it seems like his life wasn't much, but the
thing you need to know about Bobby is that he was
happy. Well, except when Dana was making him mis-
erable," she clarified. "But aside from that, he had a
good job, he was respected by his colleagues and liked
by his friends."

"I'm glad to know that. I just wish…"

"That you'd had a chance to know him," she finished for him.

He nodded.

Sadie wished there was something she could say,
some words that might somehow make him feel bet-

ter. But her mind was blank, so she followed her heart and wrapped her arms around him, holding Sullivan tight for the moment and wishing she could hold onto him forever.

Chapter Fifteen

Sadie was excited, and just a little bit sad, as she switched the 002 to 001 on her Countdown to Christmas sign. She was looking forward to Christmas, of course, but she was less excited about the post-holiday lull that followed.

"Is it really—*finally*—Christmas Eve?" Beth asked.

"It is indeed," she confirmed.

"Yay!" Her soon-to-be-partner punched both fists in the air. "I'll actually be able to sleep in tomorrow."

Sadie turned to gape at her. "You sleep in *on Christmas*?"

"As long as I can," Beth said.

"How did I not know this about you?"

"Are you saying that you *don't* sleep in?"

"As if Elvis would let me," Sadie scoffed.

"Fill her stocking with catnip," her friend suggested. "That should give you a reprieve."

She chuckled, but the truth was, even if Elvis wasn't nudging her awake at 6:30 a.m., Sadie wouldn't be able to sleep any later because she truly was like a kid on Christmas. And while she knew there wouldn't be any presents from Santa under her tree—or any presents at all, aside from the ones she would take to her mom's for their midday celebration—she didn't care. She would wake up in the morning, wrap herself in a fuzzy blanket and savor her first cup of coffee while listening to Christmas music and basking in the lights on her tree.

Sullivan hadn't said anything about his plans for the day, but she was hopeful that she'd see him at some point today or tomorrow. She'd debated the pros and cons of buying him a gift—because she certainly didn't want him to think that she expected one in return—but, in the end, she couldn't resist. Actually, there were two parts to his gift—one that she hoped he would cherish and one that she hoped would make him laugh.

"And so it begins."

Beth's ominous remark brought Sadie back to the present. She didn't have to ask what "it" was, because customers were spilling through the door.

Ninety minutes later, Sadie found a young man standing in the center of the shop, looking lost and just a little bit desperate.

"Can I help you find something?" Sadie asked.

"I hope so," he said. "My wife and I got married last February, so it's our first official Christmas together. Kelly loves Christmas—probably almost as much as you do—and we already have a 'First Christmas as Mr. and Mrs.' ornament hanging front and center on our tree."

"Marking milestones with dated ornaments is a wonderful tradition," she agreed.

"And we'll be shopping for a 'Baby's First Christmas' ornament next year."

"Congratulations," Sadie said.

He grinned. "Thanks. We're both excited about the baby, and when we were here in October to pick up some Halloween decorations, we couldn't resist looking at the Christmas ornaments. There was one we both liked—a stork carrying a baby, with the words *Coming Soon* on the front of the bundle and the year on the back."

"I'm familiar with that one," Sadie assured him.

"I wanted to buy it then, but Kelly was still in her first trimester and hesitant. But she told me that I could come back to get it if everything was okay after her three-month checkup. And it was. And at her four-month checkup, too."

"That's great news," she said, and meant it. Because while there were lots of shoppers milling around the store, it was these personal stories that she loved to hear, and the customers who shared them were the ones she really wanted to help.

"But I completely forgot about the ornament," Kelly's husband confided. "Until she made a comment about adding it to the tree on Christmas Day, and I realized that she's expecting to find that stork ornament under the tree. I really don't want to disappoint her, but I can't seem to find it anywhere. Do you have any left?"

"Follow me." Sadie led him to an adjacent room, the back wall of which was filled, floor-to-ceiling, with milestone ornaments. She carefully removed the stork from the hanger and handed it to her customer.

"That's it," he said. "I can't believe…thank you." He impulsively hugged her.

"I'm happy I was able to help."

"You didn't just help, you saved my Christmas." He couldn't seem to stop smiling. "After I check out, I'm heading straight home to wrap it."

"Or you can take advantage of our complimentary gift-wrapping service."

He grinned. "Even better."

And so it went throughout the day. Some customers knew exactly what they wanted and where to find it, while others needed a little bit of direction in both respects.

Noah came in to help out between noon and three, then Beth went home at four, but Sadie stayed open until six, as per usual, because there were always a few who wandered in later in the day.

Evy's dad was one of those late shoppers this year, though he was only coming in to pick up a snow globe that she'd special-ordered for him a few weeks earlier.

"I'm so sorry," Owen said when he finally arrived. "I'd hoped to be here earlier, but there was a plumbing emergency at the Hamptons. Apparently, their six-year-old son didn't like the sweater he was told he had to wear for dinner at grandma's, so he tried to flush it down the toilet."

"A plumbing emergency on Christmas Eve isn't fun for anyone," Sadie said sympathetically. "But why do kids always want to flush things in toilets?"

"I have no idea. And most of the time, I have no complaints—" he winked "—because they keep me in business. But I am sorry to rush in at the last minute."

"It's okay. I knew you'd make your way here eventually." She retrieved the box she'd set beneath the counter, opened the lid and carefully unwrapped the snow globe for his inspection.

"Look at that," he said, turning it carefully in his hands. "I'm always skeptical, when I choose something from a picture, but this is even nicer than I expected."

"And unique," Sadie said. Because while she sold a fair number of snow globes depicting scenes of children playing in the snow, this one was of five children—the number of Dotty's grandchildren—building a snowman with their grandmother.

"I think she'll be pleased."

He handed back the globe so that she could rewrap it in the tissue.

"Is there any chance you can wrap the box in some of your fancy paper for me, Sadie?" Owen asked hopefully, as he pulled his credit card out of his wallet.

"I'd be happy to," she told him.

As she wrapped the box, she thought about how Owen's face lit up when he talked about his girlfriend. According to Evy, her dad had dated various women after the death of her mom before realizing that the only one he wanted to be with was Dotty Brock, his longtime neighbor and friend.

Owen was about the same age as Roberta, Sadie guessed. But as far as she knew, her mom hadn't dated anyone since her husband had walked out. For more than twenty-five years, she'd been on her own. True, she'd been busy raising her daughters for the first dozen of those years, but plenty of single parents managed to make time for romantic relationships.

Had Roberta been so in love with her husband that no other man could compare to him? Or had she simply been so devastated by his abandonment that she couldn't bring herself to risk her heart again?

Sadie could certainly understand why she'd hesitate. The more time she spent with Sullivan, the more she felt herself teetering on the edge of falling for him and desperately trying to regain her balance rather than risk history repeating itself.

She pushed those thoughts aside as she added a silver bow and snowflake tag to the box she'd wrapped.

"Thanks again," Owen said.

"My pleasure." She bagged his purchase and passed it across the counter. "Merry Christmas to you and Dotty."

"And to you, too, Sadie."

She followed him to the door so that she could finally turn the Open sign to Closed—and encountered Sullivan on his way in.

"This is an unexpected surprise," she said.

"I've got a bigger surprise for you outside," he told her.

"You do?" She tried to look past him, to peek outside, but he took hold of her shoulders and gently turned her around.

"Finish up whatever needs finishing and then you can see."

So she emptied the register and locked the cash in the safe—grateful that most transactions were handled electronically these days, so she only had to make a deposit at the bank twice a week rather than every day.

"I'm finished," she said.

"Then grab your coat and let's go."

Happiness filled her heart as they walked out of Holiday House together. Not because she was anticipating the big surprise, but because she was with Sullivan and being with him made her happy.

And then he paused beside an actual horse-drawn wrought iron sleigh.

Her breath caught in her throat as she marveled over the gorgeous black Vis-à-Vis with elegantly curved runners, tufted red leather seats and shiny gold detailing. There was even a driver in a long coat with a top hat on his head.

"Want to go for a ride?" Sullivan asked.

"Are you kidding? Of course, I want to go for a ride." It was like a fairytale, except even better because he wasn't a fictional prince but a flesh-and-blood man. "But where did you find a horse-drawn sleigh?"

"It belongs to Mr. Stewart," he said, gesturing to the formally dressed driver.

Mr. Stewart tipped his hat to Sadie. "Good evening, ma'am."

"Good evening," she echoed, taking the hand Sullivan offered to help her into the sleigh.

When she was seated, he climbed up to take a seat beside her then unfolded a thick woolen blanket and spread it across their laps.

"Would you like to make any stops en route?" Mr. Stewart asked.

"Do you need to go home to feed Elvis?" Sullivan asked.

Sadie was touched that he would think about her cat, but she shook her head. "I snuck home for a few minutes before Beth had to leave."

"No stops en route," Sullivan told the driver.

"Very good, sir," he said, and set the horses in motion, making the bells on their harnesses jingle, just like in the song.

"En route to where?" Sadie asked as the sleigh glided over the snow.

"That's another surprise," he told her.

It quickly became apparent that they weren't headed toward the Flying A, which was a bit of a letdown to Sadie, who'd hoped this sleigh ride might be the prelude to a romantic seduction. But she wasn't disappointed for long, because she was cuddling with a handsome man in a horse-drawn sleigh on Christmas Eve while fluffy flakes of snow fell around them, and she couldn't imagine anything more romantic than that.

Then, as the sleigh continued toward the outskirts of town, anticipation began to build. "Are we going to Mountainview Resort?"

"Have you been there before?" he asked.

She shook her head. Though she'd driven by the up-scale resort often enough, she'd never had occasion to visit. But Lynda and her husband had celebrated their tenth anniversary there a few months back, and her friend had raved about it.

"Then this will be a first for both of us," Sullivan said.

Mr. Stewart drew the horses to a stop.

"Here we are," he announced.

They weren't at the main resort building but one of the private cabins that were scattered around the base of the mountain.

Snowy Pines Cabin, according to the sign.

An appropriate name, Sadie thought, as the pines that flanked the building were covered in a fresh dusting of snow—as was Sullivan's truck, parked in the laneway.

The cabin itself had been decked out for the holidays, with evergreen boughs hanging from the porch railing and twinkling lights beckoning in all of the windows.

"This is…*wow*," Sadie said.

"Wait until you see inside," Sullivan told her.

Her heart started to race as he took her hand again and she considered that this might be a prelude to a seduction, after all. And she was more than ready to be seduced.

"Did you want some time to relax before your dinner?" Mr. Stewart asked.

"I think we're probably ready to eat now," Sullivan

said. "Because if I know Sadie at all, she didn't stop long enough for a proper lunch today."

"There's nothing improper about a sandwich," she protested, even as her stomach growled.

Mr. Stewart chuckled. "Antony will be along shortly to serve your meal."

"Thank you," Sullivan said, offering his hand and the bill folded in his palm.

The other man tipped his hat again. "My pleasure, sir."

Taking a key from his pocket, Sullivan unlocked the door and led Sadie inside.

The interior of the cabin was open concept, the rooms divided by the placement of furniture rather than walls. A leather sectional, sturdy wood tables and a stunning fireplace defined the living room; the dining area was marked by the oiled bronze chandelier over a glossy wood table surrounded by six upholstered chairs, though it was currently set for two with fancy dishes and sparkling crystal; and stainless-steel appliances, marble countertops and glass-fronted cabinets outlined the kitchen. Every room was decorated with garlands and bows and twinkling lights. There was even a towering Christmas tree beside the fireplace.

"There's a powder room there," Sullivan said, pointing to a door just beyond the tiled entranceway. "And a full bathroom upstairs, along with another sitting area and the bedroom."

"Can I see it?"

He gestured for her to precede him up the open staircase that led to a loft with a king-sized bed beneath a skylight that allowed guests to drift off to sleep looking at the stars.

"I'm going to have to say *wow* again," Sadie said.

"I'm glad you like it."

"Like it? I might never want to leave," she warned.

He chuckled as they made their way down the stairs again. "Well, I figured you probably had plans with your mom for tomorrow, so I've only rented the cabin for one night. But if you really love it, there's no reason we couldn't come back here again."

No reason except that it probably cost a fortune, though no way was she going to say that aloud.

"I do have plans with my mom," she admitted. "Not big plans, but it's tradition for us to share a holiday meal and exchange gifts."

Sullivan took a moment to turn on the lights on the Christmas tree, then uncorked the bottle of Cabernet Sauvignon that had been set out on the counter with two glasses.

"Which is why tonight is all about you," he said, offering her one of the glasses.

"You really didn't have to do this."

"I wanted to," he said. "You spend so much time doing for others, that I wanted to do something for you."

She sampled the wine, then looked at him over the rim of her glass. "So this isn't just a fancy place to seduce me?"

The sparkle in her eyes told Sullivan that she was teasing, but just the mention of seduction was enough to have his blood heating in his veins.

"Believe me, I've given some thought to seducing

you," he confided. "But there are absolutely no strings attached to tonight."

She took a step closer. "What if I want to be seduced?"

He cleared his throat. "Is that a hypothetical question? Or a subtle hint?"

He wanted to be clear about what she wanted and what she didn't.

"Perhaps too subtle," she acknowledged. She set both their glasses on the counter again, then lifted her hands to his chest, sliding her palms over his pecs and shoulders to link them behind his head. "I want you, Sullivan."

And with those words, all the blood in his head quickly migrated south.

"Well, I wouldn't ever want it to be said that I didn't give a woman what she wanted for Christmas."

The words were whispered against her lips, and then he was kissing her. It was a kiss filled with all the heat and hunger that he'd been holding back for too long, and she kissed him back with the same desperation that was clamoring inside him.

He wrapped his arms around her, drawing her closer until her breasts were crushed against his chest and her pelvis was cradled between his hips. Holding her like this, kissing her, he was suddenly, painfully, aware that it had been almost ten months since he'd had sex. Ten months since he'd experienced the pleasure of intimacy with a woman.

But he didn't want any woman—he wanted Sadie. She was the one he thought about day and night. Hers were the kisses that teased his mind and tortured his dreams. And now that they were finally alone together, he didn't want to wait ten more minutes to strip her naked and join his body with hers.

She was apparently on the same wavelength, because she was already tugging his shirt out of his pants and sliding her hands beneath it. Her nails raked lightly over his skin, making him groan.

His heart was pounding against his ribs so hard he was certain she must be able to hear it.

Or was that someone knocking on the door?

He swore under his breath. "That'll be our dinner."

"What if I said I wasn't hungry? At least not for food?"

He would have been happy to send the server away with their meal, except that Sadie's stomach chose that precise moment to rumble again.

"I'd say you were lying," he told her.

"Okay, I'm not as hungry for food as I am for you," she clarified.

"Hold that thought," he said, moving to the door.

"Good evening." Antony pushed a service cart into the room and transferred the dishes to the dining table before lighting the candles. "Can I get you anything else?"

Sadie goggled at the amount of food on the table. "I think that should tide us over until spring."

Antony smiled and bowed. "Enjoy your dinner."

"Thank you." Sullivan offered his hand, discreetly passing a tip to the server, who earned it by immediately vacating the premises.

"I didn't think you'd want a big meal so late, so I ordered several small plates to sample," he explained to Sadie when they were alone again.

"It's perfect. And it will be just as perfect in half an hour."

"Half an hour, huh?" he asked, torn between amusement and arousal.

"Am I over- or underestimating?"

"Under," he told her. "And when I get you under me in that bed up in the loft, it's going to be a very long time before I let you go again."

Chapter Sixteen

"In that case—" Sadie reached for one of the plates "—maybe we should eat now."

He knew it was the right call, albeit a disappointing one. But they took their food and wine into the living room, where they sat by the fire, nibbling on savory sausage wrapped in flaky pastry, mushrooms stuffed with smoky bacon, crunchy bruschetta and miniature quiches. Despite having filled her plate, Sadie only sampled a few items before she set it aside to climb into his lap, hiking her skirt up to straddle his hips with her knees, and kiss him.

"You didn't eat very much," he felt compelled to point out.

"I'm not really hungry for food," she said, nibbling playfully on his lower lip.

Since she'd made the first move, Sullivan made the next one, grasping the hem of her sweater and lifting it over her head. He tossed it aside, leaving her top half clad in only a silky red bra.

"Merry Christmas to me," he murmured, making her laugh.

Then he pressed his lips to the hollow between her breasts and heard her moan.

His shirt quickly joined her sweater on the floor, evidence that their passions were quickly escalating out of control.

"There's a nice big bed upstairs," he reminded her when she reached for the buckle of his belt.

"Here works, too," she said.

He didn't argue.

In seconds, they were both naked, stretched out on a blanket in front of the fire.

Sadie couldn't believe this was *finally* happening.

After weeks of wondering if this day would ever come, it was finally here. As her hands moved over his warm, taut skin stretched over deliciously sculpted muscles, she didn't doubt that he'd been worth every minute of the wait.

He cradled her face in his palms, and she could see the reflection of the Christmas tree lights in his eyes and a heat that warmed her more than the flames crackling in the fireplace.

Had any man ever looked at her the way he was looking at her right now?

She didn't think so.

Sullivan made her feel not just desired but desirable.

Confident.

Sexy.

Was it any wonder that she'd fallen in love with him?

Wait—*what?*

No! This couldn't be love.

She knew better than to fall in love with someone else who was destined to leave her.

Didn't she?

She certainly hadn't meant for it to happen, but she'd been powerless to stop it. Because Sullivan Grainger was everything she never knew she wanted in a man.

She'd thought she was in love with Michael, but perhaps that hadn't been anything more than a teen-age crush. She'd been older and wiser when she'd met Harlow, but still her feelings for him had been nowhere near as intense as what she felt for this man.

Then Sullivan dipped his head to nuzzle her throat, and all thoughts of anyone—anything—else slipped from her mind. There was no one but him. Nothing but the here and now.

And if he wasn't likely to stay in Bronco much longer, she was determined to enjoy every minute they had together rather than worry about what might happen later. Especially when, right now, he was exploring her body with his hands and his mouth.

It was a leisurely and thorough examination, and though every caress served to further heighten her anticipation, Sadie was more than ready to stop anticipating and start experiencing the pleasure of making love with Sullivan. She moaned when he lowered his head to take one of her nipples between his lips, drawing it into his mouth to suckle it, because it felt really good. But she was ready for more than foreplay, so she guided his hand to where she wanted it—between her thighs.

He took the hint, quickly parting the slick folds of skin at the apex of her thighs. She was already wet, more than ready, and when he circled the sensitive nub with his thumb at the same time he dipped a finger inside, she shattered.

As her body shuddered with the aftershocks of her climax, he finally sheathed himself with a condom, protecting them both, then settled between her thighs. He kissed her again, their mouths merging as their bodies joined together. And it was everything Sadie had imagined. Everything…and so much more.

She wrapped her arms around him, holding onto him as he moved inside her—slow, deep strokes that drove them both toward to the edge of pleasure. Close. Closer. And finally…over.

Afterward, they dozed off in front of the fire.

When they awakened, several hours later, the fire had died down and Sadie shivered at the distinct chill in the air. But she wasn't cold for long, because Sullivan carried her upstairs to the loft where he made love to her again, so completely and thoroughly she saw stars, even with her eyes closed.

He could get used to waking with a woman in his bed, Sullivan realized. Especially if the woman was Sadie.

He'd thoroughly enjoyed making love with her—

again and again through the night—but her passion was only one of the things he liked about her. She was smart and beautiful, warm and kind, sweet and genuine and—

She shifted in his arms and tipped her head back to look at him. "Good morning."

"Good morning." He brushed his lips over hers. "Merry Christmas."

She smiled. "Best Christmas ever."

"Do you think so?" He rolled so that she was pinned beneath him. "Let's see if we can make it better."

Sadie giggled as he nuzzled her throat, sighed when he trailed kisses along her collarbone, gasped when he captured one of her already taut pink nipples with his mouth, moaned as he laved and suckled. He shifted to give the same attention to her other breast, loving the soft, sexy sounds that communicated her pleasure.

He examined every dip and curve of her body with his hands and his lips, lingering where he knew it would please them both. Finally, he nudged her legs apart and knelt between them, lowering his head to taste her intimately. She gasped, her hips lifting off the mattress, as he licked and sucked, tasted and teased, until she was writhing beneath him, whimpering with need.

Then and only then did he finally sheathe himself with a condom and bury himself deep inside her. Sadie wrapped her arms and legs around him, so they were as connected as two people could be, moving together in a synchronized rhythm that carried them both to the pinnacle of pleasure.

"Best Christmas ever," he said when he'd finally rolled away from her and managed to catch his breath.

"Isn't that what I said?" Sadie asked, sounding every bit as breathless as he.

"I'm agreeing with you." He stroked a leisurely hand down her back. "But as much as I'd love to stay in this bed with you all day—or until the New Year—check-out is in an hour."

"What time is it?"

"Just after ten."

"Ohmygod." She jolted upright. "I have to go. I need to be at my mom's house for noon."

So much for enjoying a leisurely morning in bed with the woman he lo—

He abruptly severed that thought before it could completely form.

With the woman he'd grown to care about a great deal, he amended.

And who was already pushing back the covers of the bed.

"I need a shower," she said.

"It would probably save time if we showered together," he suggested hopefully.

Sadie laughed, proving that she wasn't fooled for a minute by his offer. "I'm pretty sure it wouldn't."

He was admittedly disappointed, but he stayed where he was while she disappeared into the bathroom. He heard the water turn on and absently reached toward the nightstand for his phone to check for messages.

He'd missed three calls from his parents, and a text message.

Just wanted to wish you a very Merry Christmas.
Love you lots.
Mom & Dad xoxo

As he read the words, a fist squeezed around his heart.

He missed them both. So much.

And not just today, though the missing seemed a little sharper because it was Christmas. Because, for as long as he could remember, he'd never not celebrated Christmas with them.

But despite missing Lou and Ellie, he wasn't ready to go home. He was still trying to come to terms with the existence—and loss—of his twin brother, and he felt strongly that he needed to be in Bronco to do that.

Or maybe he was making excuses to stay, because staying meant spending more time with Sadie, and he wasn't anywhere near ready to say goodbye to her.

His thumb hovered over the keypad for a moment before he finally responded.

Merry Christmas to you, too. xoxo

He'd just set his phone back down when Sadie came out of the bathroom. The plush towel tucked between her breasts fell to the tops of her thighs, showing off plenty of smooth, creamy skin that tempted him to yank the towel away and drag her back to bed.

"I texted my mom to let her know that I'd be late," she told him. "And that I'd be bringing a guest."

And just that quickly, his fantasy evaporated.

"You want me to go to your mom's house with you for Christmas dinner?" he asked dubiously.

"Have you had a better offer?"

"No."

In fact, he hadn't had any offers until hers.

The Abernathys had assumed he'd be returning to Columbus for the holidays, and he hadn't disabused them of the notion. Because they were known to invite friends and neighbors who were on their own to join them for a holiday meal, and he hadn't wanted them to feel obligated to include him. Not only because it would make him feel pathetic, but also because he didn't want to do the whole family thing with a family that wasn't his own.

But sharing a meal with Sadie and her mom didn't sound so bad. Especially since it would mean spending more time with Sadie.

"So you'll come with me?" she prompted.

"I'll come with you," he agreed.

She smiled, and suddenly the day was a whole lot brighter.

Before they could go to Roberta's, though, they had to stop by Sadie's house so that she could feed Elvis and change her clothes and pick up her gifts for her mom and the pumpkin pie that she'd bought for dessert—apparently her usual contribution to holiday dinners.

As they headed out the door again, much to Elvis's obvious displeasure, Sadie grabbed Sullivan's hand, drawing him to a halt. "Just one more thing."

"What's that?"

She rose on her toes and brushed her lips over his. "Thank you again. For last night. For everything."

"It really was my pleasure."

She smiled. "I'd say the pleasure was very definitely mutual."

"Merry Christmas." Sadie greeted her mom with a hug and a kiss.

Roberta returned her daughter's embrace. To Sullivan she said, "I'm glad you were able to join us."

They were the right words, but there was something in her mom's tone that made Sadie think she wasn't as glad as she was pretending to be.

"I'm grateful for the invitation," Sullivan responded, well aware that it had come from her and not her mother.

"Is that the pumpkin pie?" Roberta asked, reaching for the box in Sadie's hands.

"It is." She noted, as she glanced around, that her mom had added a few more holiday touches to her modest but neat apartment. And, as usual, the pedestal table in the dining room was covered in a festive red cloth and set with Roberta's best dishes.

"Can I offer you something to drink, Sullivan?" her mom asked now.

"A glass of water would be great," he said. "Thanks."

"I'll be right back."

"I'll give you a hand," Sadie said, following her mom to the kitchen. "Can I help with anything in here?"

"Everything's under control," Roberta said. "As

soon as the rolls are warm, I'll put everything on the table."

"So why do you seem a little…on edge?"

"I'm not on edge." But her mother's short tone suggested otherwise.

"Are you upset that I invited Sullivan to join us for Christmas?" Sadie asked.

"You know that friends are always welcome at my table," Roberta reminded her.

"Then what's wrong? Because it's obvious that something is."

Her mother sighed as she opened the freezer to take out a tray of ice. "I'm just worried that you and Sullivan are becoming more than friends."

The turtleneck that she wore hid the beard burn on Sadie's throat, but it couldn't cool that heat that filled her cheeks.

"I'm not sure what we are," she said cautiously. "But I like Sullivan. A lot."

"I can see that." Roberta sounded worried.

"And I think he likes me, too."

Her mom opened her mouth as if to respond, then clamped it shut again as she popped several cubes out of the tray and into a glass.

"If there's something you want to say, say it," Sadie urged.

"I was only going to say that Dana liked Bobby a lot, too. In the beginning."

Sadie was stunned—and a little hurt—by her mother's blunt remark. "I can't believe you're making comparisons."

"I can't believe you can't see the similarities," Roberta countered, as she filled the glass with water.

"Sullivan might look like Bobby, but he's his own person, And you should know that I'm nothing like Dana."

"I do know that," her mom agreed. "But then I see the way you look at him, and it's just like Dana used to look at Bobby. And knowing how that turned out..."

"I'm going to deliver Sullivan's drink to him," Sadie said. "Then I'll come back and help you serve the food, but this conversation is over."

"You can't expect a mother not to worry about her daughter—especially when it's so obvious that she's making a mistake."

"I'm not asking you not to worry about me—I'm asking you to drop the subject."

Sullivan was looking at the collage frames her mom had hanging on the wall, filled with photos of Dana and Sadie from their early days through high school, when she returned to the living room.

"Dinner's just about ready to go on the table," Sadie told him.

"Thanks." He accepted the glass she offered, but instead of drinking from it, he set it on one of the coasters on the coffee table. "Unfortunately, it turns out that I can't stay for dinner, after all. I have to get back to the Flying A."

"Surely whatever the problem is, it can wait at least until after you've eaten," she protested.

"I'm sorry," he said. "But it can't. Please tell your mom—"

"I'm right here," Roberta said, stepping into the living room.

"Mrs. Chamberlin, thank you again for your hospitality, but there's somewhere else I need to be."

"I'm sorry to hear that," Roberta said, though Sadie knew she didn't really mean it.

"It was nice seeing you again," Sullivan told her, sounding at least a little more sincere than her mom had managed. "Merry Christmas."

"I'll walk you out," Sadie said.

"That's not necessary," he said. "I know the way."

"But—"

"I'll talk to you later, okay?"

"Okay," she agreed, wounded by his obvious brush-off.

"What was that about?" Roberta asked when the door had closed behind him.

"He said he had to go to the ranch."

"You don't believe him?"

"I think he overheard us talking in the kitchen."

"If he did, and his response was to abandon you, then maybe he doesn't like you as much as you think he does."

Sadie felt as if she'd been slapped. "Why are you doing this?"

"What is it that you think I'm doing?"

"Not being supportive of my relationship with Sullivan."

Roberta sighed. "Honey, you've known that man—what? Three weeks?"

"Why does it matter how long I've known him?"

she challenged, because she didn't think pointing out that she'd actually known Sullivan four weeks would sway her mother's opinion.

"Because you can't really know anything about him, and I'm worried that you're letting the feelings you had for Bobby carry over to his brother."

"My feelings for Sullivan aren't anything like the feelings I had for Bobby."

"Are you sure?"

"I'm sure. Bobby was my sister's husband, and I loved him like a brother."

"And you think you're really in love with Sullivan?" Roberta didn't even try to hide her skepticism.

"I don't *think*, I *know*," Sadie told her.

"I hope that's not true."

"Why would you say that?"

"Because he'll end up breaking your heart just like Bobby broke Dana's heart."

"Dana's the one who broke Bobby's heart," Sadie said. "She's the reason he died."

Her mom sucked in a breath. "That's a horrible thing to say."

"But not untrue," she insisted. "Dana was always a little bit out of control, but after Bobby went missing, she hit the bottle even harder, and I think it's because she knew who was responsible for his death."

Roberta's eyes filled with tears. "And now she's gone, too."

Sadie sighed. "I know. And I miss her, too, but revising history isn't going to bring her back."

"It was hard for her…when your dad left."

"It was hard for all of us," she reminded her mom. "You most of all."

"But Dana wasn't the same after he was gone."

"Or maybe his leaving was just an excuse for her to behave badly."

"How can you speak about your sister that way?" her mom demanded, blinking back tears.

"Because it's true. Because you worked your butt off to pay the bills and rent and put food on the table, but it still wasn't good enough for Dana. Did she ever once say thank you? No, she only ever complained about what she didn't have."

"She wanted a bigger life than the one she'd been born into," Roberta reluctantly acknowledged.

"And she set her sights on Bobby, because she thought he could be her ticket to that bigger world."

"Maybe it's the curse of Chamberlin women to fall in love with the wrong men."

"Sullivan isn't the wrong man," Sadie said, her tone resolute.

"You didn't think Michael was the wrong man at the time, did you? Or Harlow? What makes you think Sullivan is any different?" her mom challenged.

"Maybe I am making a mistake," she allowed. "And maybe I will end up with my heart broken again. I know there are no guarantees in life, but I'm willing to take a chance."

"You'd be smarter to take off the rose-colored glasses you're wearing and see him for what he is—a man passing through town and amusing himself with a pretty woman willing to share his bed."

"I'm sorry that your marriage didn't work out," Sadie said. "I'm even sorrier that you've let that experience close off your heart so completely that you can't even be happy that I'm happy."

"How happy are you going to be when he's gone?" Roberta wondered aloud.

Because she knew that was Sadie's deepest fear—that Sullivan would leave her, just like every other man she'd ever loved had left her. And it hurt that her mom would use that knowledge as a weapon against her now.

"You know what, Mom? You might be right. Maybe he will go back to Columbus." And hadn't she been bracing herself for that eventuality since the beginning? "But he's here now, and I think I'd like to spend what's left of this Christmas with him."

Sadie grabbed her coat and bag and stormed out.

Chapter Seventeen

It wasn't until Sadie exited her mother's apartment building that she realized she'd have to walk home to get her SUV before she could follow Sullivan to the Flying A, because he'd left her stranded.

Not on purpose, she was sure.

He'd simply decided to leave and hadn't thought about the fact that she didn't have a vehicle.

Thankfully, she didn't live too far from her mom—barely a fifteen-minute walk. A pleasant stroll on a sunny spring day; not so pleasant in the middle of winter.

As she trudged through the snow, she couldn't help but think that Sullivan's failure to consider her lack of transportation was all too reminiscent of Michael and Harlow, both of whom had made important choices for their own lives without considering what she wanted or needed.

Was she being unfair?

Was her mother's reminder of her romantic failures the reason she was suddenly feeling insecure about her relationship with Sullivan?

It was true that she'd only known him a few weeks. But they'd spent a lot of time together in those weeks. Shared a lot of themselves with one another. So much so that she honestly felt as if she knew him better than she'd ever known either Michael or Harlow.

Which was why she didn't believe there was any kind of emergency at the Flying A. And why she was certain Sullivan didn't want to be alone even though he'd gone off that way.

But she should have called before driving out to the Abernathy ranch, because when she got there, his truck wasn't near the barn or parked at his cabin.

Cursing her impulsivity, she dug her phone out of her pocket and pulled up his contact information, tapping the call icon. It rang five times before going to voice mail.

"Hey, Sullivan. It's Sadie. I'm at the Flying A but you're not. Please give me a call as soon as you get this message."

Then she sat in her vehicle, drumming her fingers on the steering wheel and waiting to hear back from him. But she wasn't in a mood to be patient and, a few minutes later, she sent him a text message, then waited for a response to that. Several more minutes—and a few more unanswered calls and text messages—later, she decided to go looking for him.

She tried the cemetery, but there wasn't any sign that he'd been to Bobby's grave. So she called his cell phone again, then sent another text message.

She didn't think he'd ghosted her. Though with her mother's words echoing in the back of her mind, she was forced to admit that she hadn't always had the best of luck when it came to relationships.

Maybe Sullivan had gotten what he'd wanted from her and was, right now, on his way back to Columbus. She'd spotted a bag of gifts in the back seat of his truck when she'd put her presents for her mom there and suspected he was contemplating a trip home. And if that's where he'd gone, she couldn't even be mad at him, because she'd been encouraging him for weeks to reach out to his family.

She absolutely understood why he'd been so upset to learn about his adoption and twin brother, especially at this stage of his life, but she hoped he was starting to accept that his parents' actions had been motivated by love for their adoptive son.

She wished she had a number for his parents, but even if she did, she'd be hesitant to call them. Especially as she had no real evidence that he was headed to Columbus, and she wouldn't want to alarm Lou and Ellie by implying that their son had gone missing—like his brother had gone missing more than three years earlier.

But that thought gave her another idea—a glimmer of hope that perhaps Sullivan wasn't ignoring her calls and text messages but wasn't receiving them. Because there was one place nearby that was notorious for its lack of cellular service—the base of the mountain where Bobby had fallen to his death.

So Sadie got back in her SUV and headed to the mountains.

She'd participated in the search in the weeks following Bobby's disappearance, so she didn't need a map to know where she was going, though it took her a while to get there. When she finally did, she breathed a sigh of relief to see Sullivan's truck in the parking area.

She was hardly dressed for a hike in the woods, but she had no intention of sitting and waiting for him to return. Instead, she wrapped her scarf around her throat, pulled her hat down over her ears, stuffed her hands into her mittens and stepped out into the cold.

There were all kinds of boot prints in the trampled snow—no way for her to know which might be Sullivan's. But she didn't need to follow his tracks to know where he was going.

Sure enough, she found him at the edge of the woods at the bottom of the mountain where investigators determined that Bobby had fallen.

The police had combed the area extensively without finding anything—and the volunteer search parties had gone over the same ground again and again long after the police had gone, with similarly unsuccessful results. But Sadie could understand that Sullivan would want to see the area for himself—and that on a day when families gathered to celebrate, he would be keenly missing the twin he'd never known.

"Now that I've found you, you can disregard the numerous voice mails and text messages that will show up on your phone when you've got cell service again," she said lightly.

He turned to face her then. "I didn't realize there was no service here."

"There is at the top of the mountain, but not down here." She took a few steps closer. "No one from the Flying A reached out to you, did they?"

He hesitated for just a fraction of a second before shaking his head. "The Abernathys don't even know that I'm still in town."

"They thought you'd gone home to Columbus for the holidays?"

Now he nodded.

"So why did you leave my mom's place?"

"I heard enough of your conversation in the kitchen to realize that your mom wasn't too pleased about us being together, and I didn't want to be the cause of conflict between you."

"Believe me, our conflict predates your arrival in town."

"I got the impression that you and your mom have a good relationship."

"We do. Most of the time. But we have our disagreements, too. And today's was a doozy."

"You didn't stay for dinner," he realized.

"I wasn't hungry after you left."

"You walked out on her because of me," he said, sounding unhappy about the fact.

"It wasn't because of you," she told him. "Or rather, not entirely."

"So why are you here?"

"That's because of you." She took his hand. "Because I wanted to be here for you."

"How did you know where to find me?"

"Process of elimination."

"I haven't been able to go any farther," he confided. "I think maybe I was waiting for you."

So they walked into the woods together.

"It's quite a picturesque area, isn't it?" he remarked.

"You should see it in the summer," she said, and hoped that he'd have a chance to do so. "It's a popular destination for local hikers and tourists then."

"I don't understand. If there was evidence that Bobby fell, they obviously knew where he fell—and therefore where he landed. Why wasn't his body recovered?"

"I don't know," she admitted. "But search teams scoured the whole area and came up empty."

"So what am I doing here?" he wondered aloud. "What am I looking for?"

"Closure?" she suggested.

He was silent for a long minute before he responded.

"I don't know if that's something I'll ever get," he confided, his voice anguished. "How can I find closure without ever knowing my brother? How could I have lived thirty-eight years without realizing that I had a twin? Isn't there supposed to be some kind of inherent bond between babies that share a womb?"

"I'm hardly the person to answer that question," she said. "But considering that you and Bobby were separated almost immediately after birth, I think you need to forgive yourself for not remembering him."

"There are just so many things that I wish had been different. And I thought—*hoped*—that being here would tell me something about him."

The sun was bright overhead, filtering through the trees to illuminate their path. They walked in silence for a few minutes, the crunch of their boots in the snow and the occasional cry of a bird the only sounds to puncture the quiet. Then Sadie's heel caught on something and she stumbled.

"Are you okay?" Sullivan asked.

She nodded as she crouched to pick up the fallen tree branch that had been buried beneath the snow and toss it aside.

"What's that?" he said.

"Just a broken branch."

He shook his head and crouched beside her, pointing to something that glinted gold in the sunlight. "I meant *that*."

"It looks like a ring," Sadie said.

He picked it up. "A wedding band."

Her breath caught. "Can I see it?"

He wiped the snow off the ring before offering it to her.

"Ohmygod." She swallowed. "It's Bobby's."

Sullivan's gaze sharpened. "Are you sure?"

She nodded. "The initials engraved inside—RS + DC—prove it."

"Did he still wear his ring after the divorce?"

"You're thinking maybe he stood on top of the mountain and threw the ring away?" she guessed.

"I don't know what to think."

But he was obviously trying to nurture a fragile hope.

She'd done the same thing for a long time, unwilling to believe that a good man's life had been cut tragically short. But as the days turned to weeks and then months, she couldn't imagine that Bobby had survived the fall and not contacted any of his friends to let them know he was okay. Which could only mean that he wasn't.

"The last time I saw him, he was still wearing it," she finally responded to Sullivan's question. "He said he couldn't bring himself to take it off. He didn't want to believe it was over and, for him, it wasn't."

"This is it then," he said quietly. "If he wouldn't have taken the ring off, then this is proof that Bobby is well and truly dead."

He leaned back against a tree and buried his face in his hands, a sob breaking its way out of his chest. Sadie tucked the ring in her coat pocket and wrapped her arms around Sullivan, holding him while he cried.

She cried, too. Not for Bobby this time, but for Sullivan. For everything he'd lost. Everything he'd never know.

"I'm sorry," he said when he'd managed to pull himself together.

"You have nothing to apologize for," she assured him.

"I don't usually fall apart like that."

"Then you were overdue."

He managed a smile, though the grief remained

etched deeply on his face. "We should mark the spot, in case the police want to come out here again to take another look."

She unwound her scarf and tied it around the tree, then they turned and retraced their steps to the parking lot.

"I'm glad you were here with me," he said, as they paused between their respective vehicles.

"Me, too."

He drew her into his arms and kissed her gently. "Thank you for being my friend, Sadie."

Friend?

After last night, she'd hoped they'd progressed to something more than friends—a lot more. But considering that he'd just been through an emotional wringer, she decided to cut him some slack.

"I have an idea," she said. "Why don't you come back to my place with me? We can snuggle on the sofa together, drink hot cocoa and watch Christmas movies."

"A tempting offer," he assured her.

"But one you're going to refuse," she guessed, her heart sinking.

"Only because there's somewhere else I need to be."

She wasn't going to beg, but she did feel compelled to point out, "You do know it's still Christmas, right?"

He nodded. "That's why I need to go."

Sadie knew then that he would be heading to Columbus. And while she believed it was important for him to reconcile with his parents, she couldn't help but wonder what his decision meant for the two of them—

and reflect on the fact that he hadn't asked for her input or opinion with respect to his plans.

He touched his lips briefly to hers again. "But I'll see you soon."

"I hope so," she said.

And then he was gone.

"This wasn't quite how I planned to spend Christmas," Sadie noted, as she settled on the sofa with a grilled cheese sandwich, scrolling through the channel guide with her remote until she found a favorite movie on TV.

Last night—and this morning—had been a dream come true.

How had everything fallen apart so quickly?

Not only with Sullivan but also with her mom.

She felt a little bit guilty about walking out on Roberta, but there was no way she could have stayed. She didn't need anyone—especially her mother—to tell her that she was making a mistake with Sullivan, because she didn't want to believe it could be true.

But here she was on Christmas Day, less than a handful of hours after they'd made love, alone.

As she nibbled on a corner of her sandwich, Elvis leapt onto the sofa to press her warm body against Sadie's thigh.

Not completely alone, she acknowledged, smiling a little as she stroked the cat's soft fur and was rewarded with a soft purr. Apparently her extended absences of the last few weeks were forgiven.

And maybe this wasn't so different from any other

Christmas when she'd enjoy a quiet night at home after visiting with her mom.

But tonight she wasn't feeling the effects of tryptophan because she hadn't stuck around for Roberta's traditional turkey dinner. Because there was no way she could have stayed and enjoyed a meal—not after the things they'd said to one another.

She finished her grilled cheese and paused the movie to take her plate to the dishwasher. She considered putting on the kettle to make a cup of tea, then decided to pour a glass of wine instead.

Last night, she'd fallen asleep in Sullivan's arms.

Tonight, she didn't even know where he was.

Had she done it again? Given her heart to a man who was going to leave? Who was maybe already gone?

She wanted to call him—just to say "hi." To hear the sound of his voice and make sure he was okay.

But he'd said "I'll see you soon," and she had to trust that he'd meant it.

Or maybe he'd just wanted to avoid an awkward goodbye scene.

She sighed as she dropped down onto the sofa again. "Definitely not how I planned to spend Christmas."

Elvis butted her head against Sadie's arm, reminding her that there were good things in her life and she had reasons to be grateful. And it was true.

It was also true that she wasn't comfortable with the way she'd left things with her mom. Yes, she'd been angry when she'd walked out, and she'd had reason to be. But Roberta was her mother, the only family she had left. And while it wasn't unusual for them to disagree, the words they'd exchanged today had been particularly harsh.

She couldn't call Sullivan, because she didn't want him to feel that she was pressuring him, but she could reach out to her mom.

Merry Christmas. I love you. xoxo

Roberta immediately replied to her text message.

Love you, too. So much. xoxoxo

Tears stung the back of Sadie's eyes and she felt as if an enormous weight had been lifted off her chest.

A short while later, she fell asleep on the sofa, with *White Christmas* on TV and Elvis purring beside her.

Chapter Eighteen

He felt strange knocking on the front door.

In the past, Sullivan wouldn't have hesitated to take out his key and let himself into his childhood home. But a lot had changed over the past several months. *He* had changed.

Ellie must have seen him through the window, because she yanked open the door. "Sullivan!"

Tears shimmered in her eyes as she stared at him.

His own weren't completely dry as he stared back.

She looked the same in so many ways, but different, too. There were a few more lines on her face, hollows in her cheeks, and a tentativeness in her demeanor that was completely unfamiliar to him.

He knew he was responsible for the changes. Not because he'd left Columbus, but because he'd stayed away for more than six months. Because he'd pushed his parents to the periphery of his life, rejecting them and everything they'd given him after learning that they'd made an error in judgment.

And Sadie was right, any mistakes they'd made, they'd made out of love.

He didn't have any doubts about that now.

He set down the bag of gifts he was carrying and opened his arms.

She flew into them, holding him tight, sobbing against his chest.

"You're home," she managed to choke out through her tears. "You're finally home. And on Christmas."

"Best present ever," Lou said from the doorway, sounding a little choked up himself.

Ellie didn't let go of Sullivan, but she shifted to one side to include her husband in their embrace.

"I'm sorry I stayed away so long," Sullivan said. "I just needed time to process everything."

"You don't need to apologize to us," Ellie told him. "We're the ones who are sorry."

"Here's an idea," Lou said. "Why don't we save all the recriminations and apologies for tomorrow and focus on celebrating what's left of the holiday today?"

"I think that's a great idea," Sullivan agreed, retrieving his presents and following his parents into the house.

As he discarded his jacket and boots in the foyer, he noticed that his stocking was hung on the mantel, between those of his parents, just like every Christmas for as far back as he could remember.

"You haven't opened your stockings," he noted. Then he spotted the brightly wrapped gifts under the tree. "Or any of your presents."

"We were waiting," Lou confided.

"For me," he realized.

"It didn't feel like Christmas without you," Ellie said.

"But that is turkey I smell, isn't it?"

"I had to cook the turkey," she said. "But we were going to carve it up and freeze the meat until you were home."

"I'm here now."

"And hungry?" she guessed.

Suddenly he was starving. Not just for the meal she always prepared, but for his family. Being away from home for so long had made him see how lucky he'd been and how much he'd always taken for granted.

Or maybe it was Sadie who'd made him see the truth—that he'd been loved.

He managed to swallow the ball of emotion that was lodged in his throat and say, "I could eat."

His dad chuckled. "You always could."

"Dinner's going to be a while. Why don't I make you a sandwich to tide you over?" his mom suggested.

"I can make my own sandwich."

"I know you can, but I want to do this for you."

"Thanks, Mom."

Her answering smile trembled just a little.

"I wouldn't mind a sandwich," Lou chimed in.

Ellie looked at her husband with longstanding affection. "I'll make one for you, too."

He'd missed this, too, Sullivan realized. Seeing his parents together, their obvious love and affection for one another reflected in so many ways. They'd always been his yardstick—their relationship the standard against which he'd measured his own, the reason he'd been determined not to marry until he'd found a woman that he loved as much as his dad loved his mom—and who loved him back as much as Ellie loved Lou.

He was thirty-nine years old and had yet to meet such a woman.

Or maybe, the possibility whispered in the back of his mind, *he had finally, recently, done just that.*

Could Sadie be the woman he'd been waiting for?

It was true that he'd never felt about anyone else the way he felt about her.

He'd left Bronco because he'd needed to get away. The pain of accepting that Bobby was really gone had been stark and raw and inspired in him a desperate need to see Lou and Ellie—his family. But now that he was here, he missed Sadie.

Truth be told, he'd started missing her as soon as he'd passed the town limits.

He pulled his phone out of his pocket, intending to send her a text message.

But what would he say?

Merry Christmas?

Hadn't they already covered that?

Hadn't he whispered those words against her lips when he'd awakened with her in his arms?

It was hard to believe that had only been this morning—and frustrating to accept how completely everything had gone downhill from there.

But now he was home.

Or was he?

He was glad to see his parents and looking forward to spending some time with them, but he wasn't sure that Columbus felt like home anymore.

Yes, Lou and Ellie were here. And he had a job that he'd been assured he could go back to whenever he was ready. He also had a condo that suited his needs and friends who were usually available to hang out when he was looking for company.

For a long time, that had been everything he'd wanted or needed. But now he knew that something important was missing.

Some*one* important was missing.

Sadie.

After the sandwiches had been eaten, Sullivan ushered his parents into the living room where he unpacked his presents and added them to the pile under the tree. There were three each for his mom and his dad, and another one with a tag that read,

To: Sullivan
From: Sadie
xoxo

He had no idea how her gift had gotten into the bag or what he was supposed to do with it now. It didn't seem right to open it when she wasn't there, but she'd obviously wanted him to have it today—on Christmas.

"Is everything okay?" Ellie asked.

"Yeah." He slid the gift back inside the bag. "Let's do presents."

And for the next hour, it truly felt like Christmas—comfortable and familiar and pretty darn close to perfect.

"All right then," his dad said, starting to rise from his favorite chair. "Let's get all this paper cleared away and get those potatoes mashed for dinner."

"We're not quite done yet," his mom protested.

"We're not?"

"I think Sullivan has another gift to open."

"There's nothing left under the tree," Lou pointed out.

But Ellie had obviously seen him slide the box from Sadie back into his gift tote, and she wasn't going to pretend she hadn't.

"It's just something from…a friend," he said. "I'll open it another time."

"If that's what you want," his mom said.

"But now my curiosity's piqued," his dad said. "And it's Christmas, dammit. Christmas presents are to be opened on Christmas."

So Sullivan pulled the gift out of the bag.

"Sadie, huh?" Lou said, leaning closer so that he could read the tag.

"Don't be nosy, Lou," Ellie chided.

"You're the one who brought up the gift he was trying to hide," her husband pointed out.

"I wasn't hiding it," Sullivan protested.

"So why was it in the bag?"

"I was…"

"Saving it," Ellie realized.

Which seemed to give the present more significance than he wanted to attribute to it.

"Sadie's the owner of the shop where I bought your ugly Christmas sweater and Dad's ugly Christmas sweater cookies," he said. "And she's big on theme gifts, so if I had to guess, it's probably an ugly Christmas sweater."

"Instead of guessing, why don't you open it and find out?" Lou suggested.

So Sullivan did just that, and laughed when he lifted the lid of the box. It was, indeed, an ugly Christmas sweater. The body was bright red, the front depicting a tree decorated with actual tinsel garland and colored lights that blinked when he pressed the star, per the instructions on the tag. The sleeves were patterned—but not the same pattern. One had white snowflakes falling on a dark blue background, the other had gingerbread cookies on a green background.

It wasn't just ugly—it was the ugliest sweater he'd ever seen.

His mom smiled. "I like this girl already."

His dad shook his head. "I just don't get the ugly sweater craze."

"You seem to like your cookies well enough," Sullivan noted.

"Because they're ugly but delicious," Lou said. "Your sweater is just ugly."

It was that, but he lifted it out of the box, intending

to put it on and maybe send a selfie to Sadie—and discovered there was something else beneath the sweater.

It was a framed photo of Bobby—a candid shot, obviously taken at Axle's garage while he was working. He was wearing jeans worn through at the knees and a T-shirt smeared with grease, and he had a wrench in his hand as he stood in front of a classic Mustang with its hood raised. But it was the smile on his face that squeezed Sullivan's heart.

Sadie had assured him that although his brother's life hadn't been easy, Bobby had been happy.

This picture proved it—and it was the best present she could have given him.

"That must be your brother," Lou said, examining the photo over his shoulder.

Sullivan nodded.

"Your friend must have known him well," Ellie remarked.

He nodded.

His dad cleared his throat. "I'm going to go see about those potatoes."

It was a familiar pattern, Sullivan mused. Lou ducking out of the way so that Ellie could wheedle information out of their son. Not because his dad wasn't interested, but because he knew that his wife was a much more effective interrogator. Or maybe Sullivan had never really tried to hold anything back from his mom, appreciating that she'd always been there for him to talk to whenever he needed her—and even when he thought he didn't.

"She's really special to you, isn't she?" Ellie said gently.

"I don't think I've ever felt about anyone the way I feel about Sadie," he confided.

"So why didn't you bring her home with you?"

"I wanted to. But… I'm afraid that my feelings for her might be tangled up with her relationship to Bobby."

"What was their relationship?"

"He was married to her sister, Dana. They divorced six months before he died."

"And what about your relationship with Sadie?" she prompted. "Can you tell me about that?"

So he did. He recounted their first meeting, including that Sadie had been so shocked by his resemblance to Bobby she'd fainted, followed by their second meeting at the cemetery and lunch at DJ's. He told her about the connection that seemed to grow stronger the more time they spent together, and admitted that he missed her every minute they were apart.

"I can't wait to meet her," Ellie said.

"I'm not sure that will ever happen," he cautioned.

"Why not?"

"Because if I've learned nothing else in the past year, I've at least learned to appreciate the importance of family. The only family Sadie has left is her mom, and Roberta isn't too fond of me."

Ellie frowned at that. "Why doesn't she like you?"

"Because I look just like Bobby—and Bobby broke Dana's heart."

"It's hardly fair to hold you responsible for the actions of another," she protested.

"Fair or not," he said, "I'd hate to be the cause of any tension in Sadie's relationship with her mom."

"And that's understandable," Ellie noted. "But I have no doubt that once Sadie's mom gets to know you for who you are, she'll love you almost as much as we do."

"If you really love the boy, you'll pause the interrogation to let him come to the table for dinner," Lou said, poking his head into the living room.

"Have you carved the turkey already?" Ellie asked.

"Just finished," her husband confirmed.

"Well, then," she said to Sullivan, "I guess we better go eat."

Sadie woke up early the day after Christmas with a stiff neck and an aching heart—and Elvis starting at her. Understanding her priorities, she got up to feed the cat, then checked her phone for messages.

There was nothing from Sullivan.

She felt like such a fool. Obviously she'd given her heart too quickly and to the wrong man. *Again.*

Maybe it was time to join one of those online dating services that Beth was always encouraging her to try. The problem was she didn't want to date anyone else. Because fool that she was, she was in love with Sullivan and it was going to take her some time to get over that.

Time that would pass more quickly if she was busy.

But it was December 26—the one day of the year that she had absolutely nothing to do.

She could go to Holiday House, anyway. Though the store was closed, there were always tasks to keep her busy. Tasks that might keep her mind off Sullivan.

Or would she only be assailed by memories of him there, too?

It was, after all, where they'd first met.

And where he'd first revealed that he had feelings for her, the night of the snowstorm, when he'd driven from the Flying A into town because he was worried about her.

Where he'd first kissed her.

Where they'd first slept together, even if all they'd done was sleep.

Where she'd first realized that she was falling for him.

Yep, definitely too many memories of him there.

She exhaled a weary sigh, even as she chastised herself for the self-indulgent stroll down memory lane.

There was nothing to be gained by feeling sorry for herself. And Sullivan had never made her any promises, therefore he'd never broken any promises. It was her own fault that she'd let herself get her hopes up. Let herself believe she could mean as much to him as he meant to her.

And if this was love, maybe she didn't want any part of it.

Chapter Nineteen

"I know I should have called first," Roberta said without preamble when Sadie opened the door. "But I was afraid you might not answer my call."

"When have I ever not answered your calls?"

"Never," her mom admitted. "But we've never said the kind of things to one another that we said yesterday."

Sadie nodded an acknowledgment and stepped away from the door so Roberta could enter.

"This is for you," her mom said, offering her the casserole dish she carried in both hands. "Some leftover turkey, stuffing, mashed potatoes, corn, carrots, gravy."

In other words, the meal that she hadn't stuck around to eat the day before. But her mom didn't say so, and Sadie was grateful for her restraint.

"I imagine you had a lot of leftovers," she commented, moving to the kitchen to put the food in the refrigerator.

"Not as many as I thought I would," Roberta said, following her daughter after she'd removed her coat and boots. "I knocked on 3B, because I knew Gedeon Horvath was on his own for Christmas. And he suggested that we invite Lizzie Kellner from 5D, and she asked if it was okay to bring Mabel Derring in 2C."

Sadie held the kettle under the tap to fill it with water. "I'm glad you were able to share your holiday meal with friends."

"It wasn't quite what I'd planned, but it was nice." Her mom crouched to pet Elvis. "Anyway, I should let you get on with your day."

"You don't want to stay for tea?"

"I didn't know if you'd want me to stay."

"I do." She set the kettle on the stove. "Please."

Roberta replied with a cautious smile. "Then I will. Thank you."

Sadie reached into the cupboard for her favorite teapot and dropped a couple of Holiday Wishes teabags to it.

Her mom took a seat at the table, and Elvis jumped nimbly into her lap.

"You're not supposed to be near the table," Roberta scolded with her words even as she scratched behind the cat's ears.

"She's not," Sadie confirmed. "But she's been feeling neglected and pushing a lot of boundaries these days."

"She should know by now that you always work long hours leading up to Christmas."

"She doesn't care about Christmas—she only cares that there's food in her bowl when she wants it and ear scratches when she wants those, too."

When the kettle had boiled, Sadie poured the hot water into the teapot, then carried it and the mugs to the table before retrieving a tin of Danish butter cookies from the cupboard.

"I don't need cookies after everything I ate yesterday, but I've never been able to resist these," her mom confided, selecting a round one sprinkled with sugar.

Those had been Dana's favorite, too, Sadie remembered. Not that she was going to make the mistake of bringing up her sister's name again.

After they'd sipped their tea in silence for several minutes, Roberta set her half-eaten cookie on a napkin and cleared her throat. "I want to apologize for the things I said yesterday," she finally said. "You were right. I was letting my personal experience color my opinion. I don't know your young man well enough to know if he's anything like Bobby, and I certainly shouldn't have assumed your relationship with him would follow the same course as that of your sister and his brother."

"I appreciate the apology," Sadie said.

"But I hope you know that I only said the things I did because I'm looking out for you. Because nothing hurts a mother more than her child hurting."

"I do know," Sadie agreed. "But you have to trust me to make my own decisions—even if you think they're the wrong ones."

"I'll try," Roberta promised, as she rose from the

table to carry her mug to the sink. "Thank you for the tea and cookies."

"Why are you suddenly rushing off?"

"I'm not rushing," her mom denied. "But it is almost dinnertime."

"Do you have plans for dinner?" Sadie asked.

"Well, no."

"So why don't you stay? You brought plenty of food to share."

"You don't have other plans?" her mom asked, obviously having anticipated that Sadie would be getting together with Sullivan.

"Not tonight," she said lightly.

"In that case, I'd love to stay and have dinner with you."

Sadie and her mom had just finished eating when Roberta got a text from Hazel, inviting her to be their fourth for canasta.

"You should go," Sadie urged when her mom conveyed the content of the message.

"I don't think so," Roberta said.

"Why not?"

"Because it's rude to eat and run."

"Not when you brought the food," Sadie said.

"You're sure you don't mind?" Her mom's tone was cautiously hopeful.

"Not only do I not mind, I'm happy that you have friends who include you in their activities," Sadie assured her.

"I do enjoy playing cards with them. But I have to

keep a close eye on Ron, because he won't hesitate to cheat if he thinks he can get away with it."

"Then you better get going. You don't want him to swindle your friends in your absence."

"I don't," Roberta agreed. "But I also don't want to leave you alone with all the cleanup."

"I'm not alone," Sadie denied. "I've got Elvis for company."

And maybe that response was a little too revealing, because her mom took Sadie's face in her hands and said, "I only want the best for you, baby girl."

"Your baby girl is thirty-three years old," Sadie reminded her.

"It doesn't matter how many birthdays you celebrate, you'll always be my baby girl," Roberta insisted.

"I know."

They shared a hug at the door and Sadie watched her mom drive away before she returned to the kitchen to finish tidying up.

She was filling the sink with soapy water when her phone rang and Sullivan's name popped up on the display.

She quickly dried her hands and tapped the screen to connect the call.

"Hi," she said, weak with happiness and relief that he'd finally reached out to her.

"Hi, Sadie."

She sank into a chair. "It's good to hear from you."

"I'm sorry for taking off the way I did yesterday," he told her. "There was just so much going on in my head…"

"I know it was a difficult day for you."

"But it was a great day, too," he said. "Especially the beginning, when I woke up beside you."

She felt her lips curve, because he was right—the morning had been great, and she really hoped they'd have a chance for a repeat performance very soon.

"Hard to believe it was only yesterday," she mused softly.

"Isn't that the truth?"

"So…" She swallowed. "Where are you?"

"In Columbus. At…my parents' place."

"I thought you'd probably gone home," she said, relieved to know that her instincts had been right and that he'd taken the first step toward reconciling with his family.

"Thanks for the Christmas present," he said.

"I assume you're referring to the photo."

"Actually, I thought the sweater was pretty great, too."

"It seemed to go with your holiday theme," she said lightly. "Did your mom like hers?"

"She's wearing it right now," he said. "And my dad is refusing to share his treats."

She chuckled softly. "I'm glad you made it back to celebrate with them."

"Me, too," he said. "I just wish…"

"What do you wish?"

"Never mind," he decided.

She gritted her teeth in frustration. She was happy that Sullivan had called, but she wanted him to *really* talk to her and it was obvious that he was holding back.

"You should know by now that you can talk to me about anything," she said.

"I cried on your shoulder," he reminded her. "I don't have any secrets from you."

She wished she could believe it was true, but recent events had caused her to second-guess her instincts about everything.

Still, she felt better after talking to him, though she was admittedly disappointed that he hadn't made any mention of when—or even if—he might return to Bronco.

Sadie's Holiday House opened for business again on the twenty-seventh of December with a steady influx of customers eager to see what was marked down for the after-holiday sale. Evy and Lola stopped in, too, and the little girl happily chatted about the fabulous Christmas she'd had and all the presents she got.

"And thank you, Sadie, for the Mulan doll. I'm going to take it to school for Show and Tell the first day back after Christmas."

"I'm not surprised she wants to take it to school," Evy said. "She's taken it everywhere else since she opened it."

Later in the afternoon, Sadie got an update from a liaison in the sheriff's office advising that, subsequent to her call, the woods had been searched again, focusing on the area where Bobby's wedding band had turned up, but no other evidence had been found.

On the twenty-eighth, Sadie had plans to meet her mom for lunch, but Roberta called early that morning to cancel. Ron—the notorious card swindler—had invited her to a showing of his son's work at the local art gallery and she'd decided to go. It sounded to Sadie like a date, though she knew her mom would vehemently deny it if she dared tease her about it.

Beth wasn't shy about admitting that she'd embarked on a new romance with a man she'd met online. Apparently, they'd been chatting for several weeks and she really liked him, but she was wary about meeting in person, having been catfished more than once before. However he was pushing for a real date, and Beth had decided that she was ready to give it a shot.

It seemed like love was all around—and Sadie was missing Sullivan like crazy.

The next day, she'd had barely walked in the door after work when her mom stopped by. Assuming that Roberta was there to tell her about her art gallery visit the previous day, she was taken aback when her mother opened the conversation by saying, "I heard that Sullivan left town."

Sadie felt her smile freeze on her face. "Where did you hear that?"

"I work at the diner and people talk," her mom reminded her. "And while I don't often pay attention to what they're saying, the words carry weight when it's the Abernathys talking."

"What did they say?" Sadie hadn't intended to ask, but the words spilled out of her mouth before she could stop them.

"Crosby asked when Sullivan was coming back, and Weston said he didn't know if he was."

"And, of course, you had to rush right over here to point out that yet another man I loved has left me."

"That's not why I'm here," Roberta denied, seeming shocked that her daughter would suggest such a thing. "I came to make sure that you're okay."

"I'm okay," she said, trusting that if she said it often enough, it would eventually be true. "Sullivan went home to Columbus, to see his parents, as many people do during the holidays."

"So he is coming back?" Roberta prompted gently.

"I have no reason to believe that he's not," Sadie said, unwilling to give voice to her own doubts.

"That's good, then. I just wanted to be sure that you were okay," her mom said again. "But I should have trusted that you would be. You've always been so strong."

"Do you really think so?" she asked, surprised by the offhand remark.

"I know so," Roberta said. "Not just strong but smart and determined and capable. And that's why I feel confident that, whatever happens with Sullivan, you'll be just fine."

Sadie swallowed the lump in her throat. "Now tell me about your visit to the art gallery with Ron."

Friday morning, Sadie updated the countdown sign on the door as she did every day.

360 Days Until Christmas

Which meant that it was likely to be a slow day and the few customers who wandered in would probably be bargain shoppers wanting to pick through the remnants of her post-holiday sale or party revelers looking to decorate for their New Year's Eve festivities.

"Tell me," Sadie said to Beth when they finally had a few minutes to chat, "is tonight the night?"

Her friend nodded. "I'm meeting Kevin at Doug's at seven o'clock."

"Doug's?" she echoed. "Was that his choice or yours?"

"Mine," Beth confided. "Because I trust Doug to take care of things if it turns out this guy isn't who I think he is. But I have a good feeling about this. I really think Kevin might be someone special."

"Then you should take off early to get ready for your big date," Sadie suggested.

"I was trying to figure out how to ask if I could do just that," Beth admitted.

"We've been working together long enough that you should feel comfortable just telling me," she chided.

"And I would," her coworker said, "if I needed to duck out for something important."

"You don't think this is important?"

Beth shrugged. "I'm trying not to get my hopes up too much."

"Sometimes a guy is every bit as wonderful as he seems," Sadie said.

And sometimes he disappears anyway.

She shoved that unhappy thought to the back of her mind to refocus her attention on her friend. "I'm sure you'll have a wonderful time tonight."

"Fingers crossed," Beth said, holding up her entwined digits.

Sadie smiled as she turned her attention to unboxing a shipment of cupid figurines. Sometimes she marveled over what people were willing to spend their money on, but she was happy to stock merchandise that she knew would sell—personal taste notwithstanding.

She glanced up when she heard the familiar chime of sleigh bells, a smile on her face for the new customer.

Her smile froze.

The ceramic cherub slipped from her fingers.

"You break it, you buy it," Beth teased.

Sadie barely heard the words over the buzzing in her head.

Déjà vu, she thought.

But this time, she had no doubts about who he was.

He was the man she loved.

The man she hadn't been certain she would ever see again.

"Sullivan."

Chapter Twenty

She said his name, but she didn't take a step toward him. In fact, other than her lips, she didn't move at all.

It wasn't quite the welcome he'd been hoping for, but Sullivan ventured a smile anyway. "Hello, Sadie."

His greeting seemed to unglue her feet from the floor, and she stepped over the broken pieces of figurine and flew into his arms—exactly the welcome he'd been hoping for.

He held her as tight as she was holding him, and felt as if he was home. "I take it you're happy to see me?"

"So happy," she agreed, finally drawing back to look at him. "I didn't know when—or even *if*—you'd be back."

"I told you I'd see you soon," he reminded her.

"But then you left."

Just like her father and Michael and Harlow had left, he realized.

"And now I'm back," he said. "Because I couldn't stay away. Because… I love you, Sadie."

Her lips curved. "I love you, too, Sullivan."

There was a lot more he wanted to say, but in that moment, nothing else seemed as important as kissing her—and she kissed him back as if she felt exactly the same way.

He registered the sound of applause, reminding him that they were in a public place—Sadie's place of business—and reluctantly eased his lips from hers.

"I probably shouldn't have come here in the middle of your workday," he acknowledged. "But I couldn't wait to see you."

"And I'm glad you didn't."

"What time do you close today?" he asked.

"Right now," she decided, and turned in his arms to face the smattering of customers in the store. "Thank you all for your patronage, but Sadie's Holiday House is now closed for a brief holiday."

"Closed?" one of the customers protested. "But—"

"We'll reopen again on January fourth," she promised.

"But…that's five days," a different shopper pointed out. "You've never closed for that long before."

"I've never had reason to," Sadie said, smiling at Sullivan.

There was so much that she wanted to say to him, but now that they were back at her house, words failed her. She couldn't even think, except about how fast her heart was beating and how much her body ached for his touch.

"I know we've got a lot to talk about," Sullivan said, apparently on the same wavelength. "But right now, I really need to kiss you again."

Sadie didn't reply, except to whisper "I missed you" against his lips.

"I bet I missed you more," he told her.

"I'm not sure that's possible."

And then conversation was abandoned as they left a trail of clothes on their way to her bedroom.

It was a long time later before they emerged to forage in the kitchen for something to eat.

"Slim pickings," Sullivan noted.

"I haven't had a chance to get to the grocery store since Christmas," Sadie admitted.

"You've got eggs and salsa and cheese," he said. "Any tortillas?"

She opened a cupboard and found a package that was only slightly stale.

"Perfect. We'll have breakfast burritos for dinner."

"You really do know your way around the kitchen."

"I thought I proved that with my chicken stir-fry."

"You did," she confirmed. "I'm just enjoying sitting here, watching my personal chef."

"Is that what I am to you?"

"It's only one of the many things you are to me."

"Hold that thought," he said, as he turned his attention back to the eggs in the pan.

So they had breakfast burritos for dinner, and they were delicious.

While they ate, Sullivan shared details of his visit with his parents, but it was his warm tone and relaxed posture that told Sadie, even more than his words, that he had mended fences with Lou and Ellie.

"So what are your plans now that you're back in town?" she asked, as they were tidying up the kitchen.

"Tomorrow I'm going to the Flying A to talk to Weston."

"About your job?" she guessed.

"Among other things."

"That's rather cryptic."

"If I have any news to share afterward, you'll be the first to hear it," he promised.

When Sullivan headed to the Flying A the following afternoon, Sadie decided to make an overdue trip to the grocery store.

While she was waiting in the checkout line, her phone buzzed with a text message from Evy.

I heard there was some excitement in your store yesterday…waiting on details!

What did you hear?

That Sullivan Grainger is back—and kissed you senseless in the middle of your shop.

Then you've got the details.

Hardly!

Sadie smiled at all the outraged indignation packed into that single word.

I'll fill you in later. Checking out at the grocery store now.

Come by Cimarron Rose when you're done.

I can't. I have to get my ice cream home so it doesn't melt.

Ha! It's December in Montana—your ice cream isn't going to melt.

I have to get my produce home before it freezes.

It will be okay for ten minutes.

Fine. But no more than ten minutes.

Then you better talk fast.

She was smiling as she paid for her groceries, grateful to Evy for reaching out. Because she was dying to talk to someone about Sullivan's return and she definitely couldn't talk to her mom. Not yet.

She understood why Roberta had some concerns, but she was going to have to get over them. Because if

Sadie had anything to say about it, Sullivan was going to be in her life for a long time.

Sadie spent a lot more time at Cimarron Rose with Evy than the ten minutes she'd allocated. As a result, she was still putting her groceries away when Sullivan returned from his meeting with Evy's fiancé.

"Do you realize what day it is today?" he asked.

"December thirty-first," she immediately replied.

"Also known as New Year's Eve," he pointed out.

"So it is."

"Did you have any plans for tonight?"

"I'm not really a New Year's Eve party kind of girl," she confided.

"You are tonight," he said. "Because I've got two tickets to the New Year's Eve gala at The Association."

"Oh, well, a gala is something different than a party."

"I can tell by your tone that you don't really believe it is, but I want to take my favorite girl out tonight."

Her brows lifted. "Your favorite girl? How many girls are you juggling?"

"There's only you," he promised, drawing her into his arms. "And I'm not juggling, I'm holding tight, because you're the best thing that ever happened to me and I don't want to let you go."

"You're a pretty smooth talker when you want to be," she noted.

"I only speak the truth," he assured her.

"But not always the whole truth," she said, narrowing her gaze. "You have something to celebrate, don't you? Did Weston offer you a permanent position at the Flying A?"

He seemed to enjoy working as a ranch hand and also with the Abernathys, but she didn't think it was what Sullivan, educated and trained as an engineer, had envisioned for the rest of his life. Unfortunately, there wasn't really a call for wind engineers in Bronco, but she was hopeful he might be able to find another job that would make use of his talents.

"Sullivan?" she prompted.

"Have I told you today that I love you?"

Her heart gave a happy sigh. "You have, but I'm not ever going to tire of hearing it."

"That's usually a cue to the other person to return the sentiment," he said.

"You know I love you."

"I do," he confirmed. "But I'm not ever going to tire of hearing it, either."

"And now," she said, trying to steer him back on topic, "I want to hear your news."

"What news?"

"You're enjoying this, aren't you?"

"I always enjoy being with you."

"Sullivan!"

He grinned. "Okay, yes, I have news. First, I've been offered a full-time job at the Flying A."

"That's great," Sadie said, thrilled to know that he now had another reason to stay in Bronco. But still, she was a little wary, too. "If you think that being a ranch hand will make you happy in the long term."

"Being here with you will make me happy."

He sounded as if he meant it, and the words filled her heart to overflowing.

"Second," he continued, "the Abernathys are going to install wind turbines at the Flying A, and I'll be in charge of maintaining and repairing them, as required."

That was an unexpected revelation, and one that alleviated her wariness. "So you'll be doing the same thing you did in Columbus?"

"But on a much smaller scale," he noted. "Which is why I'll also continue to help out on the ranch. But Hutch is sure that once the other ranchers see what he's doing, they'll want to get on board, too. So it could, eventually, turn into a full-time job. And if it doesn't, that's okay, too, because I'll have the best of both worlds."

She could see that he was truly happy about that, and she was happy for him.

"That is definitely cause for celebration," she said, throwing her arms around him and giving him a smacking kiss on the lips. "But if we're going to do so at The Association, I better change into something gala-worthy."

"I don't think I've ever been anywhere so fancy," Sadie confided to Evy when their men had gone to the bar to get drinks.

"Hard to believe, isn't it? Two shopkeepers from Bronco Valley ringing in the New Year at the most exclusive venue in Bronco Heights."

"I do feel a bit like Cinderella tonight—because of this dress." It was plum-colored chiffon, sleeveless and

V-necked with a wide sash studded with sparkly crystals and a long skirt that swirled around her legs when she turned.

"Who was your fairy godmother?" her friend asked teasingly. "Because that outfit is stunning."

Sadie laughed. "And now I know why you insisted I try it on when you lured me to Cimarron Rose this afternoon."

Evy had also selected a dress from her inventory. Hers was a pewter color with skinny straps and delicate flowers embroidered around the floor-length hem, and she looked absolutely stunning in it.

"Wes knew I'd feel a lot more comfortable coming tonight if you were going to be here, too," Evy confided. "So he told me about his plan to offer the tickets to Sullivan. I wasn't entirely sure that he'd be able to convince you to come, but I didn't want you to have the excuse of having nothing to wear."

"Well, I'm grateful," Sadie said, sincerely happy to enjoy a wonderful evening made even more wonderful by sharing it with friends.

When the tables had been cleared after the meal and the music started, Sullivan surprised Sadie again by rising to his feet and offering his hand.

"You want to dance?" she asked.

"Not really," he admitted. "But I want to hold you in my arms, and dancing seems to be a socially acceptable way to make that happen."

She chuckled softly. "You're such a charmer."

It turned out, he wasn't a bad dancer, either, and she was happy to spend the rest of the evening in his arms.

As the last notes of "Rock and Roll All Nite" faded away, the DJ announced that there were only ten seconds until midnight and the revelers immediately joined the countdown.

"Happy New Year," Sullivan said, as noisemakers erupted and confetti rained down around them.

"Happy New Year," Sadie echoed.

He kissed her then, long and slow and deep.

"My head's spinning a little," she admitted when they finally drew apart.

"From the champagne?" he guessed.

"From your kisses."

He grinned. "What would you say if I suggested that we go home and celebrate the New Year more privately?"

"I'd say *yes, please.*"

They celebrated long into the night and again the next morning, only leaving the bedroom when hunger demanded it. Sadie was in her robe, sipping coffee and watching Sullivan mix up pancake batter, when there was a knock at the door.

"Were you expecting company?" he asked.

"No." But she had a sinking feeling she knew who was at the door, ready to burst her euphoric bubble. "If I'd been expecting company, I wouldn't be sitting here in my robe."

"We can pretend we're not here."

"Except my SUV is in the driveway."

And Sullivan's truck was parked on the street in front of her house.

"Do you want to get dressed while I answer the door?" he suggested as an alternative.

"I'll be quick," she promised, grabbing a slice of bacon from the tray before fleeing to the bedroom.

She exchanged her robe for a pair of leggings and a sweater, then made her way to the foyer to hear her mom say, "I've obviously come at a bad time."

"It isn't a bad time," Sadie denied, and Sullivan escaped back to the kitchen. "We were just about to sit down to breakfast."

"At eleven o'clock?" Roberta sniffed disapprovingly.

"Okay, we'll call it brunch, and you can come in and join us."

"I had breakfast—four hours ago."

"Then you should be hungry for brunch now," Sadie said. "Sullivan's making pancakes."

"*Sullivan* is making pancakes?"

Sadie nodded. "And let me tell you—the man can cook."

Her mom hesitated. "Is that bacon I smell?"

"It is, indeed."

"I guess I wouldn't mind a pancake. And maybe a slice of bacon."

A few minutes later, they were all sitting around the table, enjoying fluffy pancakes with butter and maple syrup, crisp bacon and hot coffee.

"These pancakes are really good," Roberta grudgingly admitted.

"My mom's secret recipe," Sullivan told her.

"Your mom taught you to cook?"

"She did," he confirmed.

"You're close to your parents?"

"Very," he said.

A different answer, Sadie suspected, than he might have given even a week earlier, and she was pleased that his return to Columbus had effected a reconciliation with his family.

Thankfully, Roberta backed off with the questions then, instead expressing her appreciation for the meal and wishing both Sadie and Sullivan a happy New Year before she said goodbye.

Sullivan tried to find solace in his mother's conviction that Sadie's mom would warm up to him when she got to know him. The problem was, Roberta hadn't given any indication that she wanted to get to know him. And while she'd been civil enough when she was eating the pancakes and bacon he'd cooked, he knew it was going to take more than that to win her over.

And so, a few days into the New Year, when he knew Sadie would be busy at the store, he decided to stop in at the Gemstone Diner for a cup of coffee.

Roberta was obviously surprised to find him seated at a table in her section, but she was courteous enough when she asked to take his order.

When she returned with his coffee, though, she said, "I wasn't sure that you were still in town."

"I don't have any plans to leave," he told her.

"Still, from what Sadie tells me, it sounds as if there are a lot of reasons you might be drawn back to Columbus."

Her deliberately casual tone didn't fool him for a minute.

"And even more reasons for me to stay in Bronco," he said. "Not the least of which is your daughter."

Roberta's brow furrowed. "I can tell that you care about Sadie—"

"I'm in love with her," he said simply.

She glanced around the restaurant before sliding into the bench seat across from him. "I'm sure you believe you are, but your whole life has been turned upside down over the past few months, and you might not be thinking about your future rationally right now."

"My life was turned upside down," he agreed. "But Sadie helped turn everything right again."

"I don't want to see my daughter hurt."

"I'm not going to hurt her."

"You can't guarantee something like that," she protested.

He decided to try a different tack.

"At the end of February, my parents will be celebrating their fiftieth anniversary."

"Good for them," Roberta said, though she sounded perplexed by the apparent change of subject.

"My dad doesn't like to make a fuss, but my mom said that after fifty years together, she wanted a big party—so they're having a big party."

"As they should," she agreed.

"I'm thirty-nine years old, but I've never been married or even engaged because I decided a long time ago that I wouldn't make that kind of commitment until I found someone I could love as much as my dad loves my mom," Sullivan told her. "Sadie is that someone."

Roberta didn't seem to have any rebuttal to that, so he dropped a five-dollar bill on the table to pay for his coffee and walked out of the diner.

Chapter Twenty-One

"I need to ask a favor," Sadie told her mom.

It was early February, and Roberta seemed to have accepted that Sullivan was a fixture in her daughter's life—or at least learned to keep her reservations to herself.

"Anything," Roberta immediately agreed.

"Can you keep Elvis for a few days at the end of the month when I go to Columbus with Sullivan?"

"For his parents' anniversary party?"

Sadie nodded. She didn't remember mentioning the event to her mom, but obviously she'd done so.

"You know I'm happy to look after Elvis anytime," Roberta said.

"Thank you," she said, grateful and relieved that she wouldn't have to worry about her cat, because she was worried enough about meeting Lou and Ellie.

"What are you planning to wear?"

Sadie blinked. "Wear?"

"It's probably going to be a fancy party," her mom said. "Do you have something appropriate to wear?"

"I hadn't really thought about it." She had the dress she'd worn to the New Year's Eve gala at The Association, but it was probably a little too sparkly for anyone but the bride at an anniversary celebration.

"You should get something new."

"You're probably right," Sadie acknowledged. "Maybe I'll check with Evy to see if she's got anything that would be suitable."

"Why don't we go over to Cimarron Rose now?" Roberta suggested.

Sadie was certain she hadn't heard her correctly. Her mom had never been a big fan of shopping, considering it more of a chore than a pleasure. "You want to go to Cimarron Rose?"

"I like Everlee's shop," Roberta said, a little defensively.

And so, half an hour later, Sadie was walking into a changing room to try on the half dozen dresses her friend had put aside for her.

"We didn't do this often enough when you were younger," her mom remarked, as Sadie modeled the fourth dress—the one she'd already decided was a keeper. "It's a rite of passage for mothers and daughters, to shop for prom dresses together, but you didn't go to your prom."

"I didn't want to go."

"I know Michael wanted to take you."

But Sadie had known that Roberta couldn't afford to buy her a new dress, and she hadn't had anything appropriate in her closet to wear. Of course, Dana had gone to her prom a few years earlier—in a dress that their mom had worked a lot of extra shifts at the diner to pay for. And while Roberta would have done the same thing for Sadie, she hadn't wanted her to.

"Anyway, I know it isn't the same as prom, but this anniversary party is kind of a big deal, because you'll be meeting Sullivan's parents for the first time, so I'd like to buy your dress for it."

"I don't need you to buy me a dress, Mom."

"I know," Roberta said. "But it's something I want to do. Please."

Sadie drew her into the dressing room with her to ensure their conversation wouldn't be overheard by other customers. "If this is some kind of apology, it's not necessary. You already said you were sorry."

"Then let me buy the dress because it looks fabulous on you and it would make me happy to do so."

"Okay," Sadie finally relented, hugging her mom. "Thank you."

"You're welcome."

"I want to thank you, too, for making an effort with Sullivan," she said now. "I'm sure you still have concerns, and I appreciate that you've been keeping them to yourself."

"Actually, my concerns about Sullivan have been alleviated," Roberta told her.

"What changed?" she asked, curious and not entirely convinced.

"He came to see me at the diner."

He did? Sadie was stunned.

"He didn't say anything to me," she murmured.

"Maybe I shouldn't have said anything, either," her mom noted. "But it struck me, when he was there, that Bobby never would have done something like that."

She sighed. "I really wish you'd stop comparing him to his brother."

"I didn't mean it that way. What I meant is that I'm starting to see how very different Sullivan is from Bobby. And to appreciate that there are a lot of reasons you could care for him."

"I more than care for him," Sadie said. "I love him."

"I know you do," Roberta admitted. "And that's why it makes me happy to know that he loves you, too."

Sadie didn't mind that business was slow on Valentine's Day. She was happy to let the florists and chocolatiers have all the glory on February 14. And she was happy for Beth, that Kevin was turning out to be every bit as wonderful as she deserved and even taking her out for a fancy dinner tonight.

Sadie and Sullivan didn't have any big plans for the occasion, but she didn't mind. She enjoyed their quiet evenings at home together probably more than anything else, and while he'd told her that he'd be tied up at the Flying A most of the day, he'd promised to stop by to see her later.

He wandered into the shop just before five o'clock with a bouquet of long-stemmed red roses in his hand. She loved that he was traditional enough to go for the flower that represented love and passion, but she hated to imagine what he'd paid for a dozen roses on Valentine's Day.

"They're absolutely gorgeous," she said, rising on her toes to touch her lips to his. "Thank you."

"*You're* absolutely gorgeous," he said. "But I was hoping for a *yes* rather than a *thank you*."

"I think I missed the question," Sadie said.

"You did," he confirmed, lifting the end of the ribbon tied around the flowers to show her the princess-cut diamond solitaire dangling from it.

She sucked in a breath. "Is that what I think it is?"

"If you think it's a diamond engagement ring, then yes," Sullivan told her.

"Why—" She swallowed. "Why is there a diamond engagement ring tied to the flowers?"

"Because I was afraid I would lose it if I stuffed it in my pocket."

Was he actually making a joke at what was potentially the biggest moment of her life?

Or was this only a dream?

"That doesn't actually answer my question," she pointed out.

"You want to know why I have a diamond ring?" he guessed.

She nodded.

"I bought it for you. If you want it."

Did she want it?

Of course, she wanted it.

She swallowed again. "It's a beautiful ring."

"Let's try it on you," he suggested, untying it from the ribbon.

She curled her fingers into her palm as he reached for her hand. "No."

Sullivan looked stunned—and she immediately realized that he thought she was saying *no* to his proposal.

"I'm not saying that I don't want to marry you," she hastened to clarify. "I'm saying that if you want me to marry you, you have to ask the question. You don't get to show up with a ring and skip over that part."

He nodded, his relief palpable. "That seems reasonable."

But first, he reached for the hand she still held closed and brought it to his lips. He kissed her knuckles, and she melted faster than Frosty the Snowman when Professor Hinkle trapped him in the greenhouse.

"I love you, Sadie." She unfurled her fist and he linked their fingers together. "I could say those words a hundred times every day and they still wouldn't adequately express how much you mean to me.

"I came to Bronco looking for answers about my brother's life and death, but I found something even more important—I found you, and you are everything to me."

She understood what he was saying, because she felt exactly the same way. It was as if her life had two parts—before Sullivan and after Sullivan—and the after part was so much richer and fuller and happier.

"Maybe we haven't known one another very long, but I know in my heart that I'll never feel about anyone else the way I feel about you. And I know that I want to spend every day of the rest of my life with you.

"So I'm asking, Sadie Chamberlin, will you marry me?"

Now that he'd finally asked the question—and confessed his feelings in a way that made her love him even more—she should give him an answer.

And the answer was absolutely going to be *yes*, but first, she couldn't resist reminding him of a conversation they'd had way back in December.

"I love you, too, but someone once told me that being able to tolerate a partner is more important than loving them."

"I don't think I said it was *more* important," he said, a little sheepishly. "I simply remarked that tolerance can help a relationship endure."

"And do you think you can tolerate me?" she asked.

"Maybe the question should be—can *you* tolerate *me*?"

"Happily," she assured him. "The only thing I can't imagine tolerating is life without you."

"Is that a *yes*?" he prompted.

"That is an enthusiastic *yes*."

He wrapped his arms around her then and kissed her very enthusiastically.

"Now," she said, when they finally came up for air, "you can put the ring on my finger."

So he did, and it fit perfectly.

"Can we celebrate with pizza?" she asked hopefully.

"Pizza," Sullivan scoffed. "You didn't think I'd plan

something better than pizza for our first Valentine's Day?"

"Now I'm intrigued," she said. "Just give me a minute to lock up."

"I'll wait for you outside," he said.

The night was cold and quiet, the streets empty.

He guessed that most people were indoors celebrating Valentine's Day with the ones they loved, as he was looking forward to doing with Sadie. But he spotted a solitary figure on the sidewalk, illuminated by a nearby streetlight.

A man—and one who looked very familiar.

Sullivan's heart started to pound against his ribs as he recalled the rumors that had circulated months earlier alleging sightings of Bobby Stone's ghost. Except that *he* was the man folks had mistaken for his brother's apparition—and he wasn't standing in front of a mirror now.

Which could only mean…

The man took a few steps closer.

"You don't know me," he said, his baritone as eerily familiar as his features, "but I think you might be my brother."

Somehow, Sullivan managed to find his voice and respond, "Welcome home, Bobby Stone."

* * * * *

COMING NEXT MONTH FROM

HARLEQUIN®
SPECIAL EDITION™

#2953 A FORTUNE'S WINDFALL
The Fortunes of Texas: Hitting the Jackpot • by Michelle Major
When Linc Maloney inherits a fortune, he throws caution to the wind and vows to live life like there's no tomorrow. His friend and former coworker Remi Reynolds thinks that Linc is out of control and tries to remind him that money can't buy happiness. She can't admit to herself that she's been feeling more than *like* for Linc for a long time but doesn't dare risk her heart on a man with a big-as-Texas fear of commitment...

#2954 HER BEST FRIEND'S BABY
Sierra's Web • by Tara Taylor Quinn
Child psychiatrist Megan Latimer would trust family attorney Daniel Tremaine with her life—but never her heart. Danny's far too attractive for any woman's good...until one night changes everything. As if crossing the line weren't cataclysmic enough, Megan and Danny just went from besties and colleagues to parents-to-be. As they work together to resolve a complex custody case, can they save a family and find their own happily-ever-after?

#2955 FALLING FOR HIS FAKE GIRLFRIEND
Sutton's Place • by Shannon Stacey
Over-the-top Molly Cyrs hardly seems a match for bookish Callan Avery. But when Molly suggests they pose as a couple to assuage Stonefield's anxiety about its new male librarian, pretend paramour is all Callan can think about. Callan's looking for a family, though, and kids aren't in Molly's story. Unless he can convince Molly that she's not "too much"...and that to him, she's just enough!

#2956 THE BOOKSTORE'S SECRET
Home to Oak Hollow • by Makenna Lee
Aspiring pastry chef Nicole Evans is just waiting to hear about her dream job, and in the meantime, she goes to work in the café at the local bookstore. But that's before the recently widowed Nicole meets her temporary boss: her first crush, Liam Mendez! Will his simmering attraction to Nicole be just one more thing to hide...or the stuff of his bookstore's romance novels?

#2957 THEIR SWEET COASTAL REUNION
Sisters of Christmas Bay • by Kaylie Newell
When Kyla Beckett returns to Christmas Bay to help her foster mom, the last person she wants to run into is Ben Martinez. The small-town police chief just wants a second chance to explain. But when Ben's little girl bonds with his longtime frenemy, he wonders if it might be the start of a friendship. Can the wounded single dad convince Kyla he's always wanted the best for her...then, now and forever?

#2958 A HERO AND HIS DOG
Small Town Sweethearts • by Carrie Nichols
Former Special Forces soldier Mitch Sawicki's mission is simple: find the dog who survived the explosion that ended Mitch's military career. Vermont farmer Aurora Walsh thinks Mitch is the extra pair of hands she desperately needs. Her young daughter sees Mitch as a welcome addition to their family, whose newest member is the three-legged Sarge. Can another wounded warrior find a home with a pint-size princess and her irresistible mother?

Get 4 FREE REWARDS!

We'll send you 2 FREE Books plus 2 FREE Mystery Gifts.

FREE Value Over **$20**

Both the **Harlequin® Special Edition** and **Harlequin® Heartwarming™** series feature compelling novels filled with stories of love and strength where the bonds of friendship, family and community unite.

YES! Please send me 2 FREE novels from the Harlequin Special Edition or Harlequin Heartwarming series and my 2 FREE gifts (gifts are worth about $10 retail). After receiving them, if I don't wish to receive any more books, I can return the shipping statement marked "cancel." If I don't cancel, I will receive 6 brand-new Harlequin Special Edition books every month and be billed just $5.49 each in the U.S. or $6.24 each in Canada, a savings of at least 12% off the cover price, or 4 brand-new Harlequin Heartwarming Larger-Print books every month and be billed just $6.24 each in the U.S. or $6.74 each in Canada, a savings of at least 19% off the cover price. It's quite a bargain! Shipping and handling is just 50¢ per book in the U.S. and $1.25 per book in Canada.* I understand that accepting the 2 free books and gifts places me under no obligation to buy anything. I can always return a shipment and cancel at any time by calling the number below. The free books and gifts are mine to keep no matter what I decide.

Choose one: ☐ **Harlequin Special Edition**
(235/335 HDN GRJV)

☐ **Harlequin Heartwarming Larger-Print**
(161/361 HDN GRJV)

Name (please print)

Address   Apt. #

City   State/Province   Zip/Postal Code

Email: Please check this box ☐ if you would like to receive newsletters and promotional emails from Harlequin Enterprises ULC and its affiliates. You can unsubscribe anytime.

Mail to the **Harlequin Reader Service:**
IN U.S.A.: P.O. Box 1341, Buffalo, NY 14240-8531
IN CANADA: P.O. Box 603, Fort Erie, Ontario L2A 5X3

Want to try 2 free books from another series! Call 1-800-873-8635 or visit www.ReaderService.com.

*Terms and prices subject to change without notice. Prices do not include sales taxes, which will be charged (if applicable) based on your state or country of residence. Canadian residents will be charged applicable taxes. Offer not valid in Quebec. This offer is limited to one order per household. Books received may not be as shown. Not valid for current subscribers to the Harlequin Special Edition or Harlequin Heartwarming series. All orders subject to approval. Credit or debit balances in a customer's account(s) may be offset by any other outstanding balance owed by or to the customer. Please allow 4 to 6 weeks for delivery. Offer available while quantities last.

Your Privacy—Your information is being collected by Harlequin Enterprises ULC, operating as Harlequin Reader Service. For a complete summary of the information we collect, how we use this information and to whom it is disclosed, please visit our privacy notice located at corporate.harlequin.com/privacy-notice. From time to time we may also exchange your personal information with reputable third parties. If you wish to opt out of this sharing of your personal information, please visit readerservice.com/consumerschoice or call 1-800-873-8635. **Notice to California Residents**—Under California law, you have specific rights to control and access your data. For more information on these rights and how to exercise them, visit corporate.harlequin.com/california-privacy.

HSEHW22R3

HARLEQUIN
PLUS

Announcing a **BRAND-NEW** multimedia subscription service for romance fans like you!

Read, Watch and Play.

Experience the easiest way to get the romance content you crave.

Start your **FREE 7 DAY TRIAL** at
www.harlequinplus.com/freetrial.